KILLING FOR HER

ALEXIS ABBOTT

PATHFORGERS PUBLISHING

Get an EXCLUSIVE book, **FREE** just as a thank you for signing up for my newsletter! Plus you'll never miss a new release, cover reveal, or promotion!

http://alexisabbott.com/newsletter

I smile as the light breeze ruffles through the sheer white curtains at the great bay window. Glancing at the elegantly-carved mahogany clock in the corner of the room, I can squint my eyes and tell that it's just past eleven in the morning. I sit up in bed, the silken sheets rustling around me, and lift my arms up over my head to stretch. It still feels a little odd to sleep in so late, especially after a year away at boarding school where my dormitory mistress woke us before dawn every morning. Even on the weekends! One might not expect a finishing school adjacent to a luxury ski resort in Switzerland to be quite so austere about scheduling, but they are. I feel another rush of relief to be done with all that nonsense. I mean, it's not like school has ever been very difficult for me. I have always had a pretty quick mind. Math is boring, and science has way too many formulas, but I could always cobble together a good grade in the end. It was the history professor that held my interest, though, as well as the writing instructor who encouraged us to read all sorts of poetry. All of my dorm-mates despised it, but not me. The erotic imagery, the sensual descriptions of love and lust and eternity-- how could anyone hate that? But then again, I think to myself as I slide out of bed and pad over to the window, perhaps that was because all my friends had their own poetic love affairs to reflect on.

I, however, have always been too focused on school and travel and shopping to really care very much about dating. Besides, when you have moved around the world so many times as I have, you learn very quickly not to let yourself get too attached to anybody. I made that mistake once, long ago, as a little girl. It was my first time at a boarding school. I was born in St. Petersburg, but of course, my father insisted on sending me away for my education, wanting me to cultivate a more worldly perspective. So he shipped me off to London when I was only ten years old, and it was there that I learned English, croquet, and gained an eternal love for steak and kidney pies. It was also the place where I developed my very first crush.

His name was Liam, and I was smitten. Well, as smitten as anyone that age really can be. We even got to hold hands on the playground once before my father decided to take me out of school there and send me to the next academy-- all the way in Milan, Italy. Needless to say, my poor little ten-year-old heart was well and truly trampled by this move, and from then on, I have chosen to fly it solo. Never get attached, and your heart stays intact. It's as simple as that.

So far, that philosophy has served me pretty well. I am eighteen now, as of six months ago, and I have very few attachments left in this world. That doesn't bother me, though. I'm a pretty self-sufficient girl, if you ask me. I don't need a whole entourage of friends or family to keep me happy. I have some old friends from my finishing school in Switzerland that I still keep in touch with after graduating a few weeks back, but who knows how long those friendships will hold up after a long time apart? We are all going in different directions, anyway. For example, right now, I'm lounging around one of my father's vacation villas. This one is a palatial estate made of blinding white marble, made glittery by the reflection of the Black Sea just across the coastal road. If you stand out front of the place at just the right moment in late afternoon, the whole building seems to glow with the fading light of the sun. It's pretty magical, if you ask me. And considering how many beautiful, exotic places I have visited in my eighteen years on the planet, that's saying something.

I sit down on the edge of the bay window seat,

reaching up to push the window a little more open. I inhale deeply, enjoying the lovely scent of the salty sea. It's another gorgeous day here on the Bulgarian coast, and I'm already pondering what activities I can jump into today. It's springtime, so the luscious green gardens, fields, and forests that flank our property are in full bloom. Between whiffs of Black Sea breeze, I can pick up the more subtle hints of flowers blossoming, and I can hear the faint chirping of birds in the trees. When my father first informed me that he was sending me to Varna for spring vacation after graduating from my boarding school, I thought he was crazy. I mean, Bulgaria? Really? All of my equally wealthy classmates were jetting off to Greece or Monaco, and here I was boarding my father's private jet to eastern Europe. But I stand corrected now that I'm here. I understand why Daddy decided to invest in this property, after all.

I should never have questioned his judgment, to be honest. When has he ever steered me wrong? Daddy is a businessman, and a really good one at that. I don't know a whole lot of details about what exactly he does, but judging by what my peers' parents usually do for a living, I assume he must be some kind of stock market trader. Or a yacht dealer. Or a financial consultant for some big-wig company in New York City. Or maybe he's just a lucky guy who has inherited a lot of cash. I simply don't know. Every time in the past when I tried to pry into

Daddy's business dealings, he's always shooed me out of the room. Even when I put my foot down and cross my arms over my chest and pout-- which usually works in every other situation-- he just smiles and tells me it's nothing for me to worry about. Not that I'm ever worried about it in the first place. Just curious. Why should I worry? Daddy's a capable man, and I never want for anything. So who cares how exactly he makes his money, as long as the cash keeps flowing?

I suppose one could say I'm a little bit spoiled. Pampered, more like. I don't like it when people call me spoiled, because it makes it sound like I'm broken or faulty. I'm not spoiled, just well taken-care of! Nothing wrong with that. So what if I only ever stay in luxury resorts and wear only the finest, most recent designer clothes? Why should it be anybody's business how many times I have gotten to fly out to Paris for Fashion Week or to Barcelona for my favorite tapas restaurant? When you have a private jet at your disposal, you might as well use it, right? Daddy says it's fine. And that's all that matters. He's the one with the checkbook, but I'm the one with the limitless credit card.

A particularly strong breeze ruffles through my delicate vintage nightgown, making goosebumps prickle up on my legs. I giggle and smooth the skirt of it back down, heading across the room to the en suite bathroom to get ready for the day. I'm really excited, because Daddy is flying in today to join me for a few days of fun in the sun. This is how it usually works out. The school semester ends and he buys me a ticket for some gorgeous, exotic location. I never fly alone, of course. On past excursions, I have always either gone with a friend of mine or perhaps one of the many attendants and personal assistants my father seems to go through like tissue paper. It's not that he is especially difficult to work for or anything, he just likes to keep things fresh and interesting. If that means firing an assistant after only six months so he can trade her in for a newer model, then so be it.

Of course, I'm not completely oblivious. I know that's not the nicest way to conduct business. But like I said, Daddy won't let me into his world. He handles the payroll, and he handles the hiring. I just go along with whichever brand-new, bright-eyed, pretty young thing he sends me. For example, Daddy was too wrapped up in some important meeting up in Moscow to attend my graduation from finishing school weeks ago, so he sent me a sweet, supportive new friend named Tatyana to watch me walk across the stage instead. I stuck around campus for a couple days after, shuttled off to a graduation after-party in Zurich, and then hopped on a private jet with Tatyana to come here to the newly-purchased vacation estate in Varna.

I have spent so much time on planes and trains

and jets and in limousines that sometimes I feel like I might one day forget how to sit still. But it's worth it. All the moving around and making new friends over and over again has toughened me up. I'm not the shrinking violet people think I am. Sure, I'm as pampered as a princess, and maybe even a little bit sheltered, but I'm not dumb. I'm more observant than people think, including Daddy.

I blink at my reflection in the mirror, trying to decide what kind of look I should go for today. It's always exciting when Daddy comes into town. He loves me more than anything, but we don't spend as much time together as I would like. He's just a really busy guy, and I can't hold that against him. After all, its his hard work that makes all my traveling and shopping and fine dining possible. I should be grateful.

But sometimes… I do get a little lonely.

I shake that negative thought off, though, and decide on a flouncy ponytail and some winged eyeliner. I wash up, put on makeup, pull my long, honey-colored waves back into a ponytail on top of my head, and then step into my walk-in closet. I love being surrounded by such pretty things. Dresses from Rodarte, blouses from Gucci, shoes of the Louboutin or Jimmy Choo persuasion. I have enough designer handbags to fill a small museum. And my jeans? Only the finest, perfectly-tailored fits for my body. I'm pretty petite, barely a few inches over five feet, with a narrow waist and curves. Compared to some of my classmates, who were six-foot-tall, rail-thin daughters of supermodels from Oslo and Stockholm, I sometimes felt a little too curvy. But that hasn't stopped designers from sending me free goodie bags of their newest items, urging me to post photos of myself on Instagram in their clothes. It's an easy way for them to get someone like me, with a following of over five thousand, to give them free advertising.

And for me, it's just another freebie in a world that seems always eager to hand me things I want but don't really *need*. Will I turn it down, though? Of course not! I'm not immune to flattery, after all. I live a life of conspicuous leisure, and my followers expect that from me.

I put on a sundress and strappy sandals and head downstairs. Tatyana, looking both exhausted and chipper at the same time, greets me with my favorite iced coffee and a low-calorie pastry. "Thank you!" I reply happily, taking a big bite.

"You're welcome, Miss Koroleva," she says, nodding.

I giggle. "For the millionth time, you can call me Ana. We're friends, Tatyana. My dad is your boss, not me."

"Yes, Miss Kor-- Ana," she corrects herself, blushing. "By the way, your father will be here any minute. His driver called to let me know."

I jump up and let out a squeal of excitement, nearly spilling my drink. "Oh my god! Finally. I can't wait to see him," I gush.

Just then, we both turn to look at the front door as we hear the sound of tires crunching on gravel. I thrust the coffee and pastry back at Tatyana and rush out the front door to greet my father, who's just getting out of the big black sedan. He's wearing a scowl until his eyes catch sight of me running toward him. He grins and opens his arms wide.

I throw my arms around him and kiss him on the cheek, my heart racing. "Daddy! You're here! Finally!" I exclaim.

"*Da, lisichka,*" he croons, patting my cheek. "I'm here now. And we have something very important to talk about."

I look up at him with wide eyes. "Oh, we do? What is it?"

He glances around, giving the driver a curt nod. "Let's go sit in the parlor, *da?*"

"Okay, yes, of course," I say hurriedly. I rush back up the front steps and through the grand foyer. I sit down on one of the plush armchairs in the side parlor, watching impatiently as my father saunters into the room and sits down. Meanwhile, Tatyana is tasked with lugging his suitcase up the staircase. I can hear her grunting with exhaustion as the massive suitcase clunks against every stair. Daddy sits down across from me, leaning forward and steepling his fingers.

"What is it?" I ask excitedly. "Where are we going?"

He chuckles. "Oh, my dear. No. We aren't going anywhere. You are."

I frown and tilt my head to one side. "Me? Alone? Where?"

"You know your Uncle Liev, *da?*" he begins.

I nod. "Yeah, of course." He's not my real uncle, just an old friend of my father's.

"And you know that he has recently lost his *zhena,*" he continues.

I rest my chin on my hands. "Yes. You mentioned that on the phone awhile back. How is he holding up? Is he okay?" I ask. Daddy smiles wryly.

"Look at you, already so concerned for him. This is how I know you will make a perfect fit for Liev," he muses, his Russian accent clipping every syllable.

I lean back, confused. "A perfect fit?"

"*Da,* my little angel. You are of a certain age now, and I am sure you have been wondering where exactly your life will take you next," he rambles, gesticulating with his hands. My heart begins to race a little faster. I'm still unsure what he means by all this but... I have a bad feeling about where it's headed.

"Yeah, maybe college," I suggest. He clucks his tongue.

"Oh, a sweet and gentle mind like yours would be wasted on books," Daddy remarks, waving off my suggestion like it's a gnat. "I have something much more, ah, fulfilling in mind for my beautiful daughter. The light of my life. The jewel of my crown."

"Alright, Daddy, get to the point," I counter. He notices that I'm eyeing him suspiciously now, but he only chuckles and widens his smile even more, unwilling to back down.

"Okay, my *doch*, I will tell it to you plainly. Your uncle Liev is lonely. In need of a wife to look after him, to keep house, to mother his young ones."

I raise an eyebrow, feeling sick to my stomach. "And? What does that have to do with me, Daddy?" I breathe.

"Anastasia, this is a wonderful opportunity for you! To be a little wife to a powerful man. There is no better destiny for my sweet girl. The wedding will be lavish, of course, and you will live in a beautiful mansion, and you can summer in Europe-
-"

"I already summer in Europe!" I interrupt, standing up and glaring at him in complete horror and disbelief. "I'm in Europe right now!"

He holds his palms, urging me to calm down. "Da, but you will have your own estates, your own money, your own life--"

"No, I would have Liev's estates. Liev's money. Liev's life. Not my own," I correct him.

"Ah, but when you are married, it is all the same," Daddy says cheerfully.

I shake my head, my jaw dropping at the sheer lunacy of his plot.

"Daddy. Maybe you hit your head very hard and somehow this hasn't occurred to you yet but I don't *want* to marry Liev. He's--he's ancient!" I splutter, throwing up my arms.

He looks mildly offended. "Mr. Ovechkin is my age."

I roll my eyes. "Exactly."

He stands up and starts to walk over to me, but I jerk away, staring at him with tears in my eyes. "Daddy, no. I won't do it. This is insane," I tell him.

"But you are used to this lifestyle, are you not?" he asks in a quieter voice.

I wrinkle my nose. "Yes."

"And you want to continue to live this way?"

I shrug. "Sure. I guess."

"Then you will marry Liev," he says matter-of-factly.

"Is that an ultimatum?" I gasp, horrified. I can't believe this is really happening. I almost want to pinch myself and see if this is just a crazy nightmare.

"No. It is a fact," Daddy says. "You have no choice."

"Um, last I checked, I'm eighteen years old now. I'm a legal adult. I don't have to marry him if I don't want to," I insist, fighting back tears. I feel so betrayed. So confused. This isn't the father I know. My daddy would never force me to do something like this against my will. He has always taken such good care of me, given me everything I could possibly ask for, and now… well, this is totally out of character.

Daddy sighs. "That may be, but you are still my daughter. Ana, the ceremony takes place next week. In Brighton Beach."

"Next week?" I burst out. "In New York?"

He nods. "*Da*. And you will be there in a white dress. I will walk you down the aisle. And you will marry Liev Ovechkin, whether you like it or not. You will learn to love him."

"Oh, I will, will I?" I snap, tears burning my eyes. I'm so angry. So blindsided.

Daddy gives me a beatific smile and pretends to dust off his hands in a way that suggests finality. "*Da*. You will. Because I say so."

"Miss Koroleva, the stewardess asked you a question," chirps a rather nervous voice off to my right. I snap back to reality, blinking rapidly and shaking my head. I turn around to look up at the stewardess in her bright blue blazer and pencil skirt. She's smiling down at me expectantly, her perfectly-manicured hands wrapped around the handle of the refreshments cart. I smile back sheepishly, blushing a little. I peer around the stewardess to see Tatyana looking over at me. She looks both apologetic and concerned. I know she knows exactly why I'm on this private jet right now, and the reason seems to bother her almost as much as it bothers me. She has only been working for my father, and by extension, me, for a few short months, but I'm sure she's already picked up on the tension going on between the two members of my messed-up little family. Of course, she's just a personal assistant, so it's not like she has the authority to say anything about it. But I can tell it's eating her up inside. I make a mental note to talk to her about it once the stewardess leaves us alone.

"Oh, I'm so sorry. I just zoned out, I guess," I remark to the stewardess, nervously tucking my hair behind my ears. "What did you say?"

"Would you like anything to eat or drink? We have those juice boxes you like. And your father specially requested those figs stuffed with goat cheese and honey you loved so much in Greece last year," she explains. Her name plaque reads *SHELLEY*. You might think by now I would know the names of all the flight crew and staff, but to be perfectly honest, they change around so often it's hard to keep them all straight. My father has a tendency to be rather fickle in his firing and hiring practices. I learned that a long time ago. Never get too attached to a certain kindly stewardess or maid or tutor because they might not stick around for very long.

One time, years and years ago, when I was about twelve years old, Daddy sent me off to some exclusive summer camp in the south of France. It's the kind of place reserved for the children of only the most elite, well-off, flashy millionaires and billionaires in the world. We took surfing lessons in Nice, took day trip outings to the ritzy resorts and restaurants just over the border in Monaco. Not a single one of my bunkmates arrived without a limitless credit card or a thick wad of cold, hard cash to spend freely and flamboyantly over the summer. And perhaps bunkmates is a less fitting term for what we really were. Nobody bunked together. We all had our own plush, beautifully-appointed room and en suite bathroom. At twelve years old, I had a rain shower and a bidet. It was pretty lush. Anyway, despite how fancy and high-class the summer camp claimed to be, I was homesick and lonely. Now, you might think it's impossible to feel homesick when you spend more time traveling than at home in the first place, but I was twelve years old, away at camp with a bunch of French strangers, and I got my period for the first time ever. Growing up with a single father-- my mother passed away when I was still a toddler-- I was not ever prepared for this new, cruel reality. I was terrified and lonely, and I did the only thing I could think of: I called my nanny at the time, Dora.

After an hour of crying and pleading on the phone, she took a red-eye flight down to the south of France to pick me up from that lavish summer camp and take me home. She taught me how to deal with my monthly problem, assured me everything would be alright. She hugged me and took care of me as she always had for the past few years of her employment by my father. In my eighteen years of life, Dora is the closest thing to a mother I can remember. We were nearly inseparable. I loved her. And then… my dad promptly fired her.

Why did he fire her? Oh, because she gained a little weight and suddenly she wasn't the glamorous, exotic young woman he had hired to look after me anymore. And in my father's world, beauty and appearance is everything. Especially if you're a woman. So I lost Dora, and when she left, a little piece of my innocence went with her.

Not that I'm still bitter about it now or anything. That's just how things go sometimes. A lifetime of dealing with Daddy and his quirks, for lack of a better word, has taught me that.

I look up at the stewardess and say, "I'll have the figs, thank you. And do you by chance have any alcohol? I know Daddy usually keeps Grey Goose in the cabinet."

Shelley winces a little, and I can tell she's not looking forward to having to tell me no. As if I'm the one with the power to fire her for denying me alcohol while I'm underage. "Well, unfortunately, you are still under twenty-one, Miss Koroleva," she begins cautiously.

I sigh. "Not in Europe. I can drink legally there."

"We're on the way to America, though, and you can't drink there yet," she counters, looking paler and more worried by the second. I hate this feeling; the knowledge that everyone my father hires is almost as afraid of me as they are of him. No matter how patient and kind I am to the staff, they never quite stop treating me with kid gloves.

"Yeah, but Daddy's not here. The cops aren't here. I won't tell anyone," I reason with her. I give her a smile. "Seriously, it'll be fine. I don't want a lot. Just a splash of vodka in my orange juice. Besides, I haven't had one of those juice boxes since I was, like, ten years old," I giggle.

Shelley grins and tilts her head to one side, clearly considering my proposition. "I know you're not a child anymore. You're a young woman now. I just don't want to get you-- or me-- in trouble with Mr. Koroleva."

"I won't tell a soul, and neither will Tatyana. Right, Tatyana?" I ask, raising my voice a little and craning my neck to wink at her. She looks petrified for a moment at the sound of her own name, but then she smiles in relief when she realizes she's not in trouble. She gives me a vigorous nod.

"Yes, yes. Sure. Okay. Whatever you want, Miss Koroleva," she replies meekly.

"And call me Ana," I insist.

"Yes, Ana. Of course."

Shelley clucks her tongue, then shrugs and mutters, "Fuck it. You're a grown-up. You can have a splash of booze if you want. But I do have a request."

I raise an eyebrow, smirking curiously. "Sure, anything," I tell her.

She leans in and whispers in a conspiratorial

tone, "Things have been a little hectic in my life lately between this job and my boyfriend picking fights with me and stuff and I just... I'm wondering if... well--"

"You wanna do a shot with me?" I finish for you. She chuckles, blushing bright pink.

"Yes," she whispers.

I nod, grinning from ear to ear. "Sounds great."

"Sweet," she says, then stands up straight and clears her throat. "I'll be right back with your figs, Miss, and um, your *juice box.*"

I have to clap a hand over my mouth to stifle a giggle as she winks at me and leaves for a moment to retrieve our stuff. When she disappears, I see Tatyana pointedly avoiding eye contact with me. I can tell something is off with her. I mean, she's always kind of a nervous person, but this is different. I unbuckle my seatbelt and move across the wide aisle to sit down beside her.

"Hey, what's up?" I ask her softly.

She looks reluctant to tell me. I give her a nudge to the arm and she sighs. "Okay. Ana, I have to be honest with you," she begins in her faint Russian accent. "I don't feel very good about what your father has planned for you in America. It seems... wrong. I mean, you don't *want* to marry Mr. Ovechkin, do you?"

I blink in surprise at her openness. Usually Daddy's staff are too terrified of his wrath to speak their minds. My stomach turns as the reality of my new life hits me like a ton of bricks. My hands start fidgeting in my lap and I reply softly, "No. Of course not. I've been kind of in denial about it for the past few days, but I guess it's really happening. I've even tried to run off a few times in the past week, but unfortunately, Daddy has eyes and ears everywhere. I even tried to buy a plane ticket to India, you know. I thought of all places, that would be the easiest country to get lost in. I don't know what I would have done if I'd pulled it off, but... well, I was desperate. Silly, right?"

Tatyana shakes her head sadly. "No. I don't blame you. I can't believe he's really going to do this to you. I apologize if I'm way out of line here."

I lean into her and manage to summon up a weak smile. "No, no. You're totally right. It's not fair at all. I keep hoping maybe he'll change his mind at the last second or that maybe Mr. Ovechkin will back out of it himself. I just can't seem to accept the truth," I confess.

"I wish there was something I could do to help," Tatyana sighs. "I feel terrible about escorting you across the ocean to marry some ugly old man."

I shrug and pat her hand reassuringly. "No, it's not your problem to deal with. You're just doing your job. I would never hold this against you," I tell her. Just then, Shelley returns with my figs and a screwdriver. I force a grin and hold up my glass to clink with her little shot glass, and we both down our drinks with a "cheers!"

"Congratulations to the bride-to-be!" she chirps, her cheeks flushed from alcohol.

"Thank you," I reply, even though I can feel my heart shattering into a thousand pieces. Shelley leaves again and I offer Tatyana a fig. She shakes her head.

"No, thank you. I'm watching my weight," she says, patting her nonexistent belly.

I open my mouth to tell her how absurd that is, but then I remember Dora and how Daddy fired her for putting on a few harmless pounds years ago. Tatyana is smart. She knows she has to stay pretty and slender to keep her job, as unfair as that may be.

"Fair enough," I reply, chomping into a fig. I love these things, even though I know Daddy put them on the flight menu as a lame attempt to placate me. As if feeding me my favorite snack is enough to make up for the fact that he's about to marry me off to one of his crusty, ancient business buddies. It lines up pretty perfectly with his modus operandi, though: giving me gifts to make up for something. Usually, it's a trip to Spain to make up for missing my birthday. Or a new Valentino gown to atone for firing my favorite assistant. It doesn't surprise me, though. In Daddy's world, money is everything. It makes sense that he would approach parenting the same way, I suppose.

"Can I ask you a personal question?" Tatyana murmurs, biting her lip.

I nod. "Sure. Go for it."

"Has he done stuff like this in the past? Your father, I mean."

I give her a wry smile, but avert my eyes. "It's hard to talk about, you know. He's my father and I love him more than anything else in the world, but sometimes I do wonder if he has my best interests at heart. Don't get me wrong, he spoils me and gives me everything I could possibly want or need. It's just that I worry he sees me more as a pet or an asset than a daughter."

Tatyana's pretty eyes sparkle with tears momentarily, but she blinks them back. "Of course. I can see how that might be difficult. I apologize for asking."

I hate making people feel badly, so I force another smile. "No, it's fine. It's nothing new to me by now. I just wish there was some way out of this. I mean, surely Daddy knows best, but what if he's wrong this time? He says Mr. Ovechkin-- Liev-- will take care of me. Make me happy. But how can he possibly know that? What if, this time, Daddy's making a mistake? He's clever and he knows a lot more than I do about the way the world works. I can admit it: I'm sheltered. I've never even had a real boyfriend, you know."

Tatyana raises a flawless eyebrow and looks truly surprised. "Really? A girl like you with money and good looks? How is that possible?" she inquires, then immediately realizes she might have crossed a line. "Sorry. I get ahead of myself sometimes," she adds quickly.

I chuckle. "Don't worry. You won't offend me, I promise. Daddy's the easily offended one. He likes to surround himself with yes-men. But me? I find it kind of refreshing to talk to someone who won't bullshit me."

She slumps a little with relief, the tension leaving her face again. "You are much more fun to work with than Mr. Koroleva," she admits. I put an arm around her and give her a quick, tight hug.

"And it's been great getting to hang out with you, Tatyana. You'll be at the-- the wedding, won't you?" I ask, and I struggle to keep my brave face and my voice even. Lately it feels like I've been on the verge of tears. I'm usually pretty pragmatic about my emotions; I keep my feelings under wraps, just like Daddy taught me. But this whole arranged marriage thing... it's difficult to accept. And the more I talk about it, the more real it becomes.

Tatyana grins. "Of course I will be there! As long as Mr. Koroleva lets me."

"Good," I answer. "I'm going to need a friendly face in the crowd."

"Have you picked out a wedding dress yet?" she asks, trying to direct my attention away from the groom and back to something perhaps more fun to think about. It's a valiant effort on her part, but there's really no aspect of this wedding that doesn't fill my heart with sadness.

Luckily, we are interrupted by the sound of the intercom clicking on. The pilot's self-assured voice announces cheerfully, "Good afternoon, ladies and gents. We are now beginning our descent to John F. Kennedy International Airport in beautiful New York City, New York. The projected arrival time is approximately half-past-three, and the weather is a downright balmy seventy-two degrees Fahrenheit, not a single cloud in the sky as you can see from your windows now. May I ask at this time for all passengers to fasten their seatbelts and settle in for a smooth landing. Thank you for your patience and cooperation and I hope to fly again with you all soon!"

I roll my eyes and sigh, clicking the seatbelt into place as Tatyana does the same next to me. I crane around her to peer out the window, my stomach twisting into anxious knots as the private jet noses downward toward the earth.

A half hour later, Tatyana and I disembark, retrieve our luggage, and make our way through the massive, crowded airport. I'm grateful to have her with me. No matter how many times I fly, airports never get any less intimidating to me. However, just before we make it out of our gate, a tall, broad-shouldered man in dark sunglasses and a black suit stops us.

"Anastasia Koroleva?" he grunts. I go pale, terrified that he's some kind of government agent. Maybe he's here to arrest me for having vodka on the plane. But then he looks at Tatyana and makes a dismissive shooing gesture. She holds onto my arm more tightly.

"Who the hell are you?" she asks, surprising me with her ferocity.

"I am Miss Koroleva's escort. I'll take her from here," he says flatly. He reaches into his coat pocket and hands her a plane ticket. "This is yours. Terminal four, gate E-five. You're heading back to Moscow. Your services are no longer required at this moment."

I gasp. "What?"

"No, no. There must be a mistake," she protests.

He holds up a hand to silence us. "Your service is terminated from this point forward."

"But I--"

"Please leave immediately. I must take Miss Koroleva to her car," he orders. I know there's no sense in fighting. With my heart breaking yet again, I turn and give Tatyana a hug.

"I am so sorry," I whisper in her ear.

"No, I am sorry," she replies. "Take care of yourself, Ana."

"You, too," I tell her. She kisses me on the cheek,

flips Mr. Sunglasses the bird, and storms off toward her flight. The man is utterly unruffled.

"Follow me," he says.

With my heart hammering away like mad, I walk after him through the hectic airport, rolling my suitcase behind me and wondering what fresh hell I'm about to step into. I get through customs without a hitch, but my escort gets flagged for an impromptu pat-down. He glares at the agents as they surround him, and I can tell he's barely holding back his anger. He wants to come after me. He wants to guard me.

But for the moment, I'm without an escort. For once.

I look around frantically, wondering if this is possibly my last chance to make a break for it. My eyes fall across the crowds, and stop short when I see someone who makes my heart skip a beat. A tall, bulky, impossibly handsome man in all black-- much like my escort, only a million times better looking. He has inky-black hair, sharp, angular features and a powerful jaw. He ruffles his fingers back through his thick hair and then, to my amazement, he turns to glance at me. He looks like one of my father's men. My jaw drops when my eyes lock with his.

Piercing, bright blue eyes. Like two drops of the ocean lost in the crowd of angry, impatient people. He smiles at me. And for a split second, all my fear dissipates. The noise and the stress melts away as I stare at this ridiculously handsome man. He looks like the answer to my problems. I can't figure out why or how, but before I can stop myself, my feet are carrying me over to him. I'm within five feet of him when suddenly there's a huge hand gripping my arm, pulling me back. I whip around to see my escort has gotten through customs and caught up to me, and he looks annoyed. I try to rip my arm free, but his vice grip is too tight.

"Screw you," I mutter angrily.

"Just doing my job, Miss," he says, unperturbed.

When I turn back to look at the mystery man, he's gone. Along with the last remaining shred of my hope. Nobody is coming to save me. I have to face the facts.

It has been over a day, and I still cannot get her out of my head.

I knew Nestor was bringing his daughter into the country, but never in all my lifetime would I have guessed that she would have such an effect on me. She saw me. She should not have. And now, I realize that I should not have seen her, either.

She is the kind of woman who could cloud my judgment, and I know it. But it's too late now.

The sight of her coming into view was like watching an angel walk on earth. The look on her face when our eyes met hangs in my mind, following me wherever I go, making my heart pound and my blood run hot. Even at a distance, I caught the scent of her perfume, and I swear I can still catch whiffs of it on me as if we were together.

But she has my attention for more reasons than her beauty.

That young woman is an innocent, I can see it in her eyes. She may be a spoiled brat of a mafia princess, but she is vulnerable, and she has not had a hand in a single one of the heinous crimes her father has committed. I know this, because I have kept track of Nestor's every step as long as I could.

I have yet another reason to be doing what I am doing.

My big van's windshield wipers swipe away the flecks of rain hitting my car as I make my way down to the docks. But this time, though I'm winding through the same towering stacks of orderly metal shipping containers, I am not here to kill anyone.

On the contrary, I'm here to receive something.

I bring my car to a stop not far from where I'm supposed to meet with my contact. I'm wearing a heavy coat, gloves, boots, and a black beanie on this horrible day in early spring. It's still nothing compared to the long winters of Russia, but I've adjusted over the years, and I've earned the right to gripe about the weather from time to time.

Nonetheless, this is one storm I've been grateful for.

I get out of the car and make my way to the worker leaning against one of the shipping crates, smoking a cigarette. He eyes me up and down, evaluating me, and I give him a nod to confirm that I am the man he was paid handsomely to wait for.

"Pedro?" I ask, and he gives a nod in return, gesturing for me to follow him. I do so without a word. Everything has already been arranged between us, and the fewer words that get spoken out loud, the better.

I follow Pedro through the maze of shipping containers until we get to an area somewhat closed off from the rest of the docks. It's secluded from the hustle and bustle of the docks during the day, which is perfect for the business we're about to finish. It isn't the first time I've done this, but I treat every time like the first so that I never lose focus, never give myself a chance to slip up. I have seen too many comrades fall that way, and I have even exploited enough such weaknesses myself.

Pedro approaches one of the shipping containers that is subtly marked, and he points it out to me without a word, giving me a meaningful look. I nod my head at him, and I reach into my pocket slowly. His eyes widen, but I hold up my hand with a friendly smile, silently assuring him that I'm not about to pull a gun on him. He pauses, and he relaxes when he sees that I'm pulling a fat roll of cash out of my pocket. He even chuckles a little, and I give him a curt nod as we pass each other and I hand off the bribe to keep him happy and quiet. He slips a key into my hand in return. Pedro leaves the area, off to keep his family a little better fed while I am left to deal with the contents of the shipping container.

I hate having to do things this way, but it is our only option. And failure is not an option, not for what I have in mind. It will all be worthwhile once I can put my plans into motion.

I unlock the heavy padlocks on the container, and the crate creaks loudly as I wrench open the latches that allow me to pull the heavy, half-rusted doors open. Light floods the interior of the cave-like shipping container, revealing the inside of it.

The stony faces of nearly twenty young men stare back at me, squinting their eyes in the dim daylight as they get the first breath of fresh air they have tasted in nearly a week. They look sweaty and sleep deprived, some of them thinner than I would like, but all of them muscular and tall. Most are no older than twenty, but a few look closer to my age. There are cheap blankets strewn all over the floor of the container that the men have been sleeping on and using for warmth, and one of them is still wrapped up tighter than a babushka. The foul smell coming from the crate tells me there's a chamber pot somewhere in there, and I can see the scraps from their rations pushed into a rough pile in the corner of the crate.

These conditions could not be less ideal, but I have seen far worse in my day. I make eye contact with each and every man present before I crack a smile.

"Comrades," I say in Russian, their native tongue as well as mine, "welcome to America."

Grins split on the faces of some of the men, who embrace each other or clap hands together, and I gesture for them to follow me out of the container.

"Get some fresh air, stretch your legs a little," I say. "You've earned it." I watch each and every one of them file out, and I size them up as they go. But the last man out doesn't seem interested in moving with the crowd. Instead, he steps right up to me, a big smile on his scraggly, bearded face. I peer at him for a moment, and then he speaks.

"Nikolai, it hasn't been *that* long, has it?"

At the sound of his voice, recognition hits me, and my eyes widen.

"...Maxym?" I say, hardly able to believe I would ever say that name again. But to my surprise, my old friend starts laughing, and we embrace each other in a strong, solid hug, so shocking that even I can't help but laugh. "Good god, Maxym, what are the chances?"

"You old bastard," he growls, clapping me on the shoulder as we break apart. "You don't think your name has been going around back home in Russia? When I got wind of what you were doing, I pulled some strings to jump on this ride to America. Beats fighting for petty jobs in Moscow before another ride to prison, don't you think?"

"You're still as clever as ever," I say. "Good. You're going to need it. All of you," I add, addressing the rest of the group of people. "We have a lot of work ahead of us, but first thing is first--we need to get you relocated. It will be a tight fit in the van, but we're only making one trip. I'll get you all to the safehouse, where you can get settled and recover from the journey. For now, take a few moments. You're safe here. Stretch a little."

While the men gather their scarce belongings and chatter amongst themselves, Maxym steps aside with me, arms crossed as we survey the group together.

"More than I expected," I remark. "Many more. That's good."

"All eager for work," Maxym says, nodding. "Your recruiters in Russia have served you well."

"Tell me a little about these men," I say. "What kind of stock am I dealing with?"

"All prisoners, as you ordered," Maxym says, grinning, "including yours truly."

I crack a smile. "What did they finally get you for, hm?"

"I got overzealous," he says, putting his hands on his hips. "One of my cousins is at the bottom of the Volga River because he botched a car theft from some rich fuck who was making money off drug running. So I killed the snotty bastard and got caught. No regrets."

"That's the Maxym I know," I say, chuckling. "And these men, similar stories?"

"Ha! I'm soft compared to most of these bastards," he says. "Most of these are soldiers of other bratva who got thrown under the bus by their bosses. All have done hard time, usually put away for gang violence. There's not a single man here who doesn't have blood on his hands, and they had nowhere else to turn once they were rotting behind bars. Your offer couldn't have come at a better time."

"That's good," I say. "Very good."

"Has the plan changed at all?" he asks. "The longer we linger, the harder it will be to keep the element of surprise on our side."

"I have everything under control," I say. "In fact, we may be acting sooner than I expected. There has been a new development that interests me."

"Oh?"

"We'll talk in the van," I say, "I've kept you all waiting long enough."

We hastily make our way back to the van I brought with me, and the big vehicle groans and sinks under the weight of all the men piling into it like sardines. The smell is spectacular, but I fortunately have a large safehouse ready for them across the city where they can eat and clean themselves up.

"You picked a fine day to make this happen,"

Maxym comments as the rain starts to get heavier, and the waves crash against the docks one after another. "Sunny America, just as advertised, eh comrade?"

"Waiting for the storm was the best chance of going undetected," I say as I move around to the driver's door and climb in. Maxym gets in the passenger's side, and we pull off. "After all this time, I'm not willing to let something like an overzealous border patrol agent ruin all our plans."

"I don't blame you," Maxym says, leaning back in his seat and taking a deep breath, rubbing his eyes. "I'll be honest, we had bets going on whether or not you'd still be alive by the time we arrived."

"Thanks for the vote of confidence," I say with a dark chuckle.

"Don't get me wrong, I'm glad we weren't met with a storm of bullets when those doors opened," he says. "But few men ever dare think about going up against the men you're dealing with, much less put a plan into action."

"My brother," I say, "if you're surprised, then you don't know me at all."

"I feel like I don't, after all these years," he laughs, ribbing me, and I can't help but smile. "Did you ever think that when I picked that fight with you in the schoolyard all those years ago, we'd end up as comrades?"

"Never," I admit. "I thought I'd kill you for

stealing those cigarettes from me before we dropped out."

"I did you a favor," he says with a hearty chuckle. "That habit would have killed you, and the teacher would have whipped your ass for having gotten a hold of smokes at your age."

"You sound like my sister now," I shoot back.

"I could tell you what your sister sounded like last night," he jokes, and I punch him in the shoulder as both of us laugh. Maxym and I have known each other since we were children, and this kind of back and forth has always been how we greet each other. It all started with a fight when we were barely ten years old, but we grew on each other.

We decided long ago that conflict is how we became friends, so we might as well keep it up.

But time has a way of moving people around. When I immigrated to the United States, Maxym stayed behind, and we lost touch with each other. I assumed I would never see him again, like so many other people I left behind in Russia, but fate has other plans for us, it seems.

"Most of this bunch come from Siberia," Maxym says, gesturing to the back of the van. "I had just been transferred there when word went around through your recruiter."

"Word didn't spread too loudly, I hope," I say.

"No, he was careful," he clarifies. "None but the disenchanted. The dregs who don't have the kind of support other bratva soldiers get behind bars. Our bosses cast us off to rot, so everyone in this van has a chip on his shoulder and wants somewhere to let it out."

"Good," I say. "They'll get their fill of that and then some, when it's time."

"What about this new development, then?" he asks.

I frown as I turn onto the highway, making my way across the city through traffic, keeping as low a profile as a van full of people can.

"There is a girl. Nestor's daughter," I say in a lower tone, not wanting people besides Maxym to hear me.

Maxym raises an eyebrow. "And who is she to you?"

"That's not important," I lie. "It's who she is between Nestor and Liev Ovechkin that matters. She's going to be pawned off as a political marriage to him. And it's happening very soon. She just got flown in yesterday."

"Bullshit," Maxym says, eyes wide. "You're positive?"

I give a cold nod. "I'm rarely wrong, comrade. I don't have to tell you why this is a problem, do I?"

"Not at all," Maxym says, groaning. "So what, you deal with this girl, and-"

"Not like that," I say, cutting him off. "She's just as

much of a victim in all this as...everyone else," I say, leaving off what is in my mind.

Maxym doesn't say anything, but he nods understandingly. He is one of the few people in the world who likely knows why I do what I do. He knows why I have spent so many years piling lies upon lies, playing the Korolevas and the Ovechkins in equal parts, straddling the fence like a shadow. And he knows that I am justified in everything I am doing.

He knows that I'm going to make them pay for what they did to my parents.

"Be careful, comrade," Maxym says in a low tone, looking at the road ahead of us. "Don't let your emotions cloud your judgment."

"My emotions are what keep me going against my better judgment, it's too late for that," I say grimly. "You remember that pact we made when we were teenagers, don't you?"

Maxym smiles, and he gives a slow, understanding nod. "No regrets. Only action."

"No regrets," I repeat. "Only action."

ANASTASIA

I have set foot in a lot of over-the-top manors and palatial estates, but this… is one for the books. I'm sitting in the back seat of the black limousine that collected me from my ritzy hotel room on the Upper East Side, watching as the scenery outside my windows changes from nice to ritzy to uber-rich as we leave the thick of the big city and head out across Long Island. The driver is taking me to visit my fiance, the indomitable Liev Ovechkin, at his gaudy mansion. Apparently he lives and works out of the estate, so he's agreed to see me in between business meetings this evening. That doesn't surprise me much, since Daddy tends to operate the same way. He's never not working. Even when he's lounging around on some white-sand beach with a margarita in his hand, he's got a cell phone in his other hand, chattering away in rapid

Russian. I can't remember the last time we went on a vacation together that didn't consist mostly of Daddy making promises to do fun activities with me like surfing or rock-climbing, only to cancel at the last second and send one of his assistants to go with me instead. There are lots of reasons I suppose I could be resentful toward my father, but I can't exactly hold all of that against him. After all, it's his hard work and devotion to whatever mysterious work he does that allows to live the lavish lifestyle we enjoy in the first place. So if I have to put up with sharing my dad's attention with an endless stream of investors and consultants, then so be it. Every vacation home is also an office, and every pleasure cruise doubles as a business expense.

No big deal, though. Not compared to this newest, most recent transgression, anyway. I still can't quite wrap my head around it. I am getting married. And not to some handsome, romantic, charming guy my own age. No. Daddy is marrying me off to one of his oldest friends, and I do mean *oldest* in every sense of the word.

The car rolls to a stop in front of a gigantic, fifteen-foot-high wrought iron gate, half-shrouded by palm trees and thick underbrush. I raise an eyebrow.

"Palm trees? In New York?" I scoff. "Really? Who does he think he's kidding?"

The driver glances at me in the rear view mirror

and I can see just the faintest, quickest flicker of a smile cross his face. I know he wants to agree with me, but he won't. I don't blame him, either. It's true what I told Tatyana: my dad has eyes and ears everywhere. He might just brush off my sass, but for an employee? Well, let's just say he's fired better employees for less.

The driver steps out of the limo and walks up to a big black box to the left of the gate. He pops it open and holds down a rectangular button with two of his fingers. I roll down the window to listen as the box emits a high-pitched beep. Then an electronic-sounding voice speaks.

"Enter gate code or call for assistance," says a robotic female voice. I wrinkle my nose. I have always had a weird aversion to fake, electronic female prompters. Something about it makes me think of some dystopian sci-fi future in which every gross, handsy man has a lady-shaped robot to do his bidding.

The driver presses the button again and clears his throat to announce, "I'm here with Anastasia Koroleva to meet with her future husband, Mr. Ovechkin."

I shudder involuntarily at his words. *Future husband.* Just another cruel reminder of why I'm here in New York instead of heading off to some college or university in Europe like I had hoped for. I used to dream about growing up to become some kind of international diplomat or something. Do a job that matters. Find a career that helps other people, not just me. I have traveled so much and picked up bits and pieces of so many foreign cultures and languages during the years. I always assumed that once I reached this age, I could finally put some of that experience to good use. Pay back all the luxuries and privileges I have been gifted by virtue of my birth. But not anymore. As it turns out, my father has a different idea in mind for me. To live a much less impactful or important life. To play housewife to some rich old toad. My fate has been sealed, and it's not a pretty one to look at.

There's a pause, and then a more human-sounding voice replies, "Come on in."

The black box beeps again, and the imposing gate slowly swings open. The driver closes the box and slides back behind the wheel, pulling through. The car tires crunch over gravel as we make our way up the long, ostentatious driveway to the front of the Ovechkin manor. I have known Liev since I was a little girl, and I grew up referring to him as Uncle Liev from time to time. He has always been a sort of hovering presence in my life, sometimes accompanying Daddy and me on our trips around the world. One time when I was thirteen, Uncle Liev showed up to my tap dance recital at my boarding school in London. Daddy wasn't able to make it because of a prior work engagement, so he sent trusty old Liev in his place. At the time, I was only a little put out by the shoddy replacement, but Liev got back in my good graces by taking me out for ice cream after the curtains closed.

Perhaps that is why our betrothal bothers me so deeply. I don't think of Mr. Ovechkin as an equal, as someone who could ever be a partner or, god forbid, a lover. He's more like a substitute father figure. An old man with deep pockets and a smug smile who could buy me nice things but would never dare touch me in a non-chaste manner.

Although, I remind myself grimly as the limo rolls to a halt, I guess I will have to get used to the idea of that. I can't bear to think about it right now, though. I have to put on a brave face. It's what Daddy would ask me to do, and I'm nothing if not a daddy's girl in the end.

The driver turns off the engine and steps out to open my passenger-side door and offer me his hand. I hesitate, taking a moment to breathe deeply and still my racing heart. It doesn't really work, though. There is really no good way to prepare for something like this. The driver says softly, "You can handle this."

I look up at him, surprised. He gives me a gentle smile and a nod. "Come on."

I reluctantly take his hand and he helps me out, shutting the door behind me. I follow him up the marble front steps of the manor to the gigantic, carved mahogany entrance. There are two marble lions flanking the door like the world's most ineffectual guard dogs, and I have to roll my eyes again at how over-the-top and stupid it is. I have seen enough villas and mansions by now to have developed a pretty damn discerning eye, and I can tell this place was built by the kind of man who has way too much time, money, and ego on his hands. More chutzpah and insecurity than he knows what to do with. It strikes me as odd that in all the years I've known Liev, I have never been to his house. But then again, I haven't spent a whole lot of time at our own home in Sands Point, either. We have a gorgeous, massive, historic mansion on four acres there. But I haven't spent more than maybe a month or two in that house at any given time in years.

The driver knocks at the front door, and immediately I hear the rustling of busy feet coming down the hallway to answer it. I bite my lip, my hands fidgeting behind my back as I wait. Moments later, a butler dressed in a full traditional black suit regalia answers the door. He looks wan at first, but when he realizes who I am, his eyes widen.

"Miss Koroleva, what a pleasure to meet you," he says in a crisp British accent as he bows to me. Oh my god. Of course, Liev has a real-live British butler complete with a bushy mustache and slicked-back salt and pepper hair. I'm actually a little surprised he doesn't have a monocle, to boot.

I nod and smile nervously, wanting to rush past all the usual boring niceties. I'm not in the mood to play high-society princess right now. In fact, the sooner I can get this meeting over with, the better. But still, I have never been the kind of girl to be rude to the staff, so I reply in a deceptively bright and chipper tone, "Nice to meet you, too. What's your name?"

The butler looks a little taken aback by the question. That's not a great sign.

"Gregory Chilton," he says, "at your service."

Yikes. Even Daddy doesn't program his staff to introduce themselves like stock characters in some outdated British period drama. Or at least, he doesn't do that in front of me.

"What would you prefer I call you?" I ask pointedly.

He looks visibly uncomfortable with the question, but replies quietly, "Anything you like, Miss Koroleva. As the future lady of the house, I defer to your authority."

My eyes widen and I can feel my heart sinking down into my stomach.

"What about Greg? Is that okay?" I ask, trying and failing to stay cheerful.

"As you wish, Miss," he replies.

"Right. Okay. Well," I say awkwardly, turning back to the driver. "I guess I'll be done here in a little while."

"I will wait outside for you," he answers. Then, in a lowered voice, he adds, "Good luck."

"Thank you," I tell him earnestly. In my head, I think, *I'm going to need it.*

The driver leaves and I step into the massive foyer, staring around at the gaudy interior. The ceilings are vaulted, the walls decorated with mismatched paintings by various well-known artists, but something about their haphazard, unharmonious jumble makes me think these paintings were not purchased by someone with a discerning eye for art, but by someone who simply wanted a status symbol. The bragging rights of getting to point to the wall and say, *I own that. A museum could make use of it, but I own it.*

Again, not a great sign of things to come. "If you'll follow me, Miss, the master of the house is waiting for you upstairs in his study," says Greg.

The master of the house? Oh boy. I follow him up the grand spiral staircase flanked with gold-trimmed banisters and more lurid paintings. A chandelier made of what looks like Swarovski crystal dangles overhead like a bright, expensive Christmas ornament. Greg leads me down a long hallway filled with yet more paintings, this time bearing the faces of old-timey men. Busts of generals and lieutenants, wealthy aristocrats with high collars and smug expressions. I wondered if the men depicted were ancestors of Liev himself. It wouldn't surprise me, not in the context of this ridiculous house.

Finally, we come to a door at the end of the hall, and Greg raps lightly on the smooth wood. A familiar, annoyed voice from inside barks, "What is it?"

Greg grimaces slightly and replies, "Your future wife has arrived, Mr. Ovechkin."

I hear the shuffling of papers, and then the distinctive grunt of an older man getting up off of a piece of furniture, and then heavy footsteps. The door swings open and Liev's round, bulldog-like face splits from ear to ear in a wide grin. He's dressed in a business suit, one nearly identical to a suit my father owns. I can just picture the two of them going shopping together at some high-end menswear boutique. Yelling at the tailor, demanding new patterns and cuts. It's not a nice image.

"My dear little *myshka!*" he exclaims, opening his arms wide. "What a lovely sight you are for a lonely old man."

I force my lips to shape into a smile. "Hi, Mr. Ovechkin. It's b-been a while."

His beady black eyes flit over to the butler and he glares. "Well? What are you standing around for? Get out and do something useful. This is a party of two, Chilton."

I nearly gasp at how rude he is to the butler, but Greg takes it all in stride. He bows away, murmuring a string of apologies. Liev rolls his eyes and shakes his head, then puts his fat, fleshy hand on the small of my back to usher me into the room.

"Come, come. Sit with me, my dear," he says, shutting the heavy door behind us. I find myself glancing desperately at the three wide windows behind his gigantic cherrywood desk, as though I might jump out of them to escape. The view from the windows is impressive. Even in the fading light of evening, I can see a manicured lawn with fountains and topiary in the shapes of birds. It reminds me of a shoddily-recreated Versailles, without any of the charm.

I sit down in one of the cushy armchairs, my eyes drawn instantly to the massive set of ivory tusks jutting out of a plaque on the wall. Beside them is a mounted tiger head, and what looks to be the head of a rhino. Liev follows my gaze and chortles, pointing at it as he settles into the chair beside me. "Ah, you've noticed my hunting trophies. That rhino in particular was a difficult hunt. A worthy adversary, but I got him in the end," he brags.

"Aren't those endangered or something?" I ask, squinting.

He shrugs. "Oh, those scientists are always cooking up some new reason to deny a man his right to go head to head with a beast. But don't you worry, I have the best connections. I know where to find the safari guides who look the other way. Perhaps that could be an idea for our honeymoon, *myshka*! Have you ever been on safari?"

It takes all of my willpower not to grimace. I simply smile and shake my head. "No, I have not. Guns aren't exactly my favorite."

"Nonsense, nonsense. We'll have you shooting in no time," he laughs, brushing off my reluctance like it's a piece of dust. "Anyway, I wanted to bring you here so we could meet before the wedding and discuss, ahh, *business*."

"Business?" I repeat, raising a brow.

He nods, rubbing his hands together. *"Da.* Your father tells me you have just finished school, and he was wondering what should be the next chapter of your life."

"Yes. I was planning to go to university, study international relations," I tell him, warming to the subject. "I've always had an interest in politics and diplomacy and--"

He holds up a fat finger and clucks his tongue. "Oh, how ambitious you are, my little busy bee. But don't you worry about all that. No need to fret over making money and building a career. Not anymore."

"But I would like to--"

"I said, not anymore," he repeats more emphatically, staring hard at me with those black, piggish eyes. I realize how futile it is to tell him what I want. I close my mouth and he smiles, putting the "charm" back on. "As I was saying, you have grown into a beautiful young woman. No longer the skinny little girl whose tap dance recital I attended years ago. Oh, you were so cute in that leotard, your little curls in pigtails. I knew even back then that you would be a truly phenomenal woman once you matured."

I can't tell if he means it as a compliment or not. I give him a forced smile.

"Th-thank you?" I murmur.

"No, thank *you*, Anastasia. And thank your wonderful father for arranging this! You know, when my wife passed away some time ago, I was understandably crushed. Don't be jealous, Anastasia," he quips, giving me a wink that could curdle milk. "I did love her for many years. But fate had other plans. I was so lonely. I have great wealth. Much freedom and many privileges that other men could only dream of. But even the most independent and powerful man has one particular need that cannot be satisfied by money alone. Can you guess what that may be?" he asks, leaning forward.

What I want to do is vomit all over his shiny loafers, but instead I just shake my head, feigning ignorance. Liev reaches over and grabs my hand with his squishy, wrinkly one. It takes all my strength not to jerk away from him.

"That need is best fulfilled by a young, nubile body," Liev says, utterly without shame. "And you, my little *roza*, are just what the doctor ordered."

I'm speechless, staring at him open-mouthed and

wide-eyed. Luckily, he doesn't seem at all worried by my reticence. He steamrolls onward. "Throughout time, there has been no greater partnership than a powerful man and a beautiful woman. What I can bring to the table is strength, knowledge, wealth, connections. I can fly us anywhere, procure for us any luxury you may desire. And what do you have to offer in return? Beauty. Youth. Innocence. Where I am hard, you will be soft. Where I am harsh, you will be gentle. You see? It is like yin and yang. A partnership for the ages."

I can only nod slowly, taking it all in. My mind is overflowing with fear and disgust, but I have to make it through this meeting somehow. Liev seems pleased. "See? You are already in agreement! Ah, I knew you would be a perfect fit for me, Anastasia. Sweet and gentle. Agreeable. Everything a man could want. And your body? Well, let's just say that the animals on our honeymoon safari won't be the only ones on display," he chuckles.

"So this is really happening?" I mumble breathlessly.

He grins. "*Da, da.* I can hardly wait. It's just like my good friend Theodore Harrington always says: you must pluck a flower as it blooms, for once it wilts, there is no use for it. And you, my little minx, are in full bloom," he croons.

There's a faint crashing sound from across the house, and Liev's warm expression instantly morphs into a scowl of irritation. He stands up and dusts off his jacket, then says to me, "Stay here. It seems that my new maid is just as incompetent as she is unattractive. Give me a moment to set her straight."

He storms out of the room, already cursing and shouting. As soon as he's gone, I hop up with half a mind to jump out the window after all. The name he mentioned sounds familiar to me: Theodore Harrington. Then it hits me like a ton of bricks.

That's the name of the congressman whose name has been in the news lately for allegedly groping an underage waitress at his private yacht club. I have heard whispers of his bad behavior through the usual girl-gossip channels online, and he's long been considered a creep, all-around. It does not bode well that my future husband is buddies with a guy like that.

A stack of papers on the desk catches my eye. When we first arrived, I heard him shuffle some stuff around on his desk. Almost like he was rushing to hide something. Suddenly, my curiosity overwhelms me. I hurry over to the desk and extract the stack out from under a big glass paperweight and start hastily scanning the documents for anything interesting. At first it all looks like a bunch of business jargon and legalese until I notice the name Theodore Harrington again-- along with the name of an airline.

The Bloom Express.

I furrow my brow in confusion as I pick it up. Again, the name sounds oddly familiar, and not in a positive way. I read over the document and realize it's a printout of an email correspondence between Harrington, Liev, and some other men. They are discussing an upcoming "pleasure cruise" on a private jet. I read further down and have to clap a hand over my mouth when I see the phrases "barely legal" and "mile-high club."

That's more than enough for me to put my suspicions together.

Liev Ovechkin is a bad guy. A pedophile. An abuser.

And soon? He'll also be my husband.

A moth lands on my face as I sit so perfectly still that I look like a statue, lying on my stomach in thick hedges. It rests for a moment before taking off again, nothing but my body heat giving away the fact that I am not part of the layout of this estate's gardens. I am wearing all black clothing, from my balaclava to my sweater, gloves, pants, and boots. My outfit is made of materials that will not catch on the branches and twigs that conceal me when it's time for me to run, because that time *will* come--and soon.

Even the sniper rifle in my hands is jet-black.

It has been four hours.

I have lain perfectly still in this exact same position, watching the window. For what feels like an eternity, I have waited for my prey, more patient than the wolf or the hawk. It seems so simple now, just waiting in the bushes for my target to appear, but a world of preparation went into the simple action. As I told Maxym, I am taking no chances, taking no risk for failure with this operation.

It isn't every day that I get a shot at assassinating Liev Ovechkin. And I'm here to make sure it's the only shot I need.

Four hours ago, I set my plans in motion.

Every morning, the security guard who covers the night shift of the Ovechkin estate grounds leaves his apartment in his junker of a car to get coffee at the same cafe. Weeks before, I watched him on this routine, day in and day out. I've even sat in the cafe, out of sight, listening to him on the phone. He complains about his job to his friends, his mother, and his girlfriend. Liev is a miserable man to work for, and the morning routine is his only time to vent about it. The guard works long hours and gets paid next to nothing for it.

It was the easiest thing in the world to stop him this morning at that cafe and have a chat with him. It was even easier to bribe him a year's salary to ensure that he and his fellow guards not pay attention to this particular part of the estate gardens at this time of night. All I asked was a brief window of opportunity. The guard readily agreed. Money changed hands. The deal was made.

I didn't plan on having to act so soon, but time is

working against me now. And the prep work I did beforehand paid off.

Four hours ago, I parked my car outside this estate in Nassau County wearing a denim jacket over my clothes and a tattered snapback to hide my face. With my rifle stored in a case, I made my way on foot to the estate, keeping to the shadows and staying out of sight of the many security cameras the stunningly rich people in the area own. I had already cased the estate many times over the weeks.

I know Liev Ovechkin's daily routine better than he probably knows it himself.

He wakes up late, usually well into mid-morning or sometimes noon. Every day, he enjoys a sumptuous brunch out on the back patio, usually forcing whatever poor girl shared his bed last night to pretend she isn't terrified of him while sipping on mimosas and getting ready for whatever else he might ask her to do. He then goes back inside for most of the afternoon, and from my interviews with the security guard and others like him who work for the man, I know that he spends most of this time either handling business calls, meetings, or sticking his prick into the girl from the night before, if he likes her. In the evenings, he takes his dinner at home on weekdays and out at business dinners on the weekends before retiring to his estate here, sometimes to indulge in drugs and sex workers, other times to get drunk in his office and rail at whatever subordinates are at the estate at the time.

There are other details I have memorized over the weeks, just by watching. I know which wines he prefers, what foods he is allergic to, when his dry cleaning comes and goes, and how long it takes him to get downstairs to one of his cars. There are a dozen different ways I have killed him in my mind, following my plans through step by step in my imagination.

And walking through each plan to its conclusion brings me special joy each and every time. I am not a sadist. I usually take little joy in killing. I always pick my own contracts, and the men whose lives I take are only the worst of the worst, those who the world is far better off without.

But this one is personal.

It isn't just about the politics. It isn't even about my own fight to the top of the ladder in Brighton Beach. No, it's about the hundreds of men's and women's lives he has thrown under the bus and into the gutter over the years. It's about what he did to my parents. It's about how he helped *create* the monster I am.

My eyes are on the window of his office. Most evenings, he makes his way to the window and enjoys a smoke or a glass of wine, peering out onto the gardens, often while making a phone call. Liev doesn't need to be subtle, walking down the road to make business calls. Everyone in his home knows who he is and what he does. He's a powerful enough man that he both doesn't need to hide and does need to stay safe.

But he is smug. He thinks himself safe. And best of all, with the marriage negotiations happening between him and Nestor, he is distracted.

The time is soon. I can feel it. I lower my face to the scope of my sniper rifle, and I put the crosshairs on the window. Finger on the trigger, I wait.

Seconds pass. Minutes. My ears are keen to everything going on around me, every insect crawling through the leaves and the traffic in the distance.

When a pair of hands thrust the window open, my heart beats just a little faster, and my body tenses. I focus my gaze through the scope and get ready. My target appears in the window.

I take my finger off the trigger, and my jaw falls open.

It's her.

The girl from the airport is at the window. She looks every bit as beautiful as I remember her, perhaps even more so. In the faint moonlight, her face is even more lovely, her eyes shining with more passion...but not the kind of passion that makes my heart stir with desire. There is fear in those eyes-- fear and determination.

Just what are you planning, Miss Koroleva?

She peers out the window and looks down, biting her lip. Through the scope, I can see the emotions running through her mind: fear, anxiety, desperation, determination. I realize what she's about to do before she even begins, even though I pray that she isn't so foolhardy as to think she can really make it work.

But before my eyes, I see her climb up onto the windowsill and turn around, sticking a leg down to try and find purchase on the stonework below.

I am stunned by her audacity.

That stone wall is one that would give even me pause before I tried to scale it, one way or the other. The stonework is hardly suited for such climbing, and too much of it is smooth and easy to slip on. Somehow, I doubt that she has had the same kind of training I have for such situations. But I must admit, her smaller size could work to her advantage.

That isn't the case, however. From the moment she nearly slips and falls on her first step, I can tell she's no secret gymnast about to make her way down with speed and dexterity. This is the act of a desperate woman, and to try something as foolish as this, she must be desperate indeed.

Given what she's running from, I can't blame her. In fact, I find her bravery admirable. What a puzzle this woman is proving to be.

I watch her hands and feet find their way around the stonework as she tries to lower herself down in all that expensive clothing. I'm still stunned that she seems to be just winging this. I know what a person with a plan looks like, and I can't see that kind of drive in her. She's improvising, because she has nothing else to turn to. Hell, if I hadn't bribed the guards to stay away from this area, an alarm would already be going up.

She scrambles down a few steps, and I watch her pull the window shut behind her. That's clever. It might only buy her a few seconds, but a few seconds can be the most valuable thing in the world at times like this.

No sooner has she shut the window than I see one of her feet leave the stone it was resting on, and when she lets her weight back down, she loses the purchase she had a second ago.

Every muscle in my body acts at once.

I burst from the hedges like a maniac, abandoning my covert hiding spot, abandoning the plan. I don't know quite why I act as I do, but I know I must act.

Because the girl is falling, and there's about ten feet of nothing but air to the stone below.

I leave my rifle behind. It can't be traced to me, so the only thing that I will lose from this is the cost of one of my favorite weapons. My legs carry me quickly through the brush, every second passing like a full minute as I watch her body fall. She puts her hands to her mouth as she falls, not wanting to scream and raise an alarm prematurely. At least she has good sense, but it will all be in vain if I can't get to her in time.

I don't even perceive the obstacles between me and her. Every instinct in my powerful body works together to clear the distance between us. There is a low stone wall between the patio her small frame is headed for and the rest of the garden. I put a leg up on it and kick myself up into the air as she falls.

For a split second, I can hear her quick, sharp breath as she braces to hit the ground.

My arms wrap around her mid-air, and I intercept the fall, turning my back to hit the stone wall of the house with the girl in my arms.

Her whole body is frozen solid as a rock, her eyes wide open and staring up. She must have no idea what just happened to her. She might even be expecting that she is dead. I look down at her and give her a shake, trying to get her attention. Shaky eyes turn to me, and her face goes pale as she recognizes the eyes looking down at her. I can sense her body tensing up, about to scream, so I reach up to my balaklava and pull the mask off, glowering down at her.

"You," she breathes, her voice thin and fragile.

"We need to run," I growl. "Now."

ANASTASIA

    I stare up into my savior's face, stunned to silence. The same enchanting, blue, oceanic eyes that caught my attention at the airport are gazing down at me now. His black hair is slightly ruffled from pulling off his balaclava, and I follow the sharp cut of his cheekbones cast in shape contrast by the light of the moon and shadows of the night. There's a wildness to him that unsettles and intrigues me at the same time. Like I'm staring into the eyes of a mighty beast, and I'm not sure yet if he's a protector or a predator.

Something tells me he is the former, though. Especially since I now know acutely what a true predator looks and feels like. Liev is a predator. I am his prey. Or at least, I will be if we don't get the hell out of here fast.

The world is silent except for our breathing, and

the thumping of my heartbeat. It seems as though the entire atmosphere has frozen, crystallized in place as we look at each other. The recognition in his eyes warms my heart even though I know how foolish that sounds. I don't really know this man. He's a stranger. I saw him once in a crowded airport and that's it. We didn't even get a chance to exchange words or names, and yet, I have the strange sense that he knows me. Not just on a shallow, surface level, but he knows my heart. My soul. My intentions. My fears. He knows why I'm here, why I just fell from the window. He knows how much danger I am in, and how much danger he is in for catching me. I'm dangerous to know. I realize that. And the second I fell into his arms, he became a target, as well.

But something about the ferocity, the fire crackling in his blue eyes tells me that this man, my mysterious protector, is more than capable of handling it. And that's a good thing, because suddenly, I hear a terrible sound that breaks the silence.

A creaking noise.

The door opening to a room above us, the room from which I just escaped. My eyes go wide and I gasp, but the man instantly puts his hand over my mouth. His jaw tenses up and the fire in his eyes intensifies. He gives me an almost imperceptible shake of his head, warning me not to make a sound.

But it gets worse. I hear loud music blasting from the room, and it gets louder when the window squeaks open. My heart sinks down to my stomach and my blood runs cold in my veins. Liev. He's opening the window.

I hear him bark my name. "Anastasia?"

He sounds angry and confused. We have seconds before he glances down and figures it out. We are slightly obscured by the hedges, but we have almost certainly left an impression in the pristinely-kept foliage. Again, Liev calls out my name, this time louder and more insistent.

"Anastasia!"

I close my eyes tightly, too terrified to look. My mystery man stands stock-still, holding me in his arms. And then, through the dark veil of my eyelids, I can detect a bright light passing over us. A floodlight. Shit.

The man from the airport hisses in my ear, "Take my hand. Run."

In one swift, fluid movement he sets me on my feet, grabs my hand, and yanks me along behind him as he takes off through the thick hedges, weaving in and out of the topiary bushes with me stumbling a step behind. My heart is racing, my shorter legs struggling to keep up with my much more athletic escort. He moves with the speed and agility of some apex predator, a silky black panther or a wolf, darting in between the flashes of light. I whimper with terror as the adrenaline floods through my veins, and we're moving so quickly it feels like my heart might explode. My entire chest is on fire. I'm not particularly out of shape, but I am no athlete either, and I can't keep up with him. He tightens his grip on my hand, just the same, dragging me along as the sharp twigs and thorns of the hedges scratch at my clothes, skin, and hair. I feel a lock of my long, wavy hair get ripped out of my scalp to dangle from a thorny branch behind us and I can't help but yelp in agony and surprise. My designer blouse is being ripped to shreds, my feet aching in my hot pink Balenciaga slingback pumps, which are absolutely not made for this kind of frantic escape. Every cell in my body is aflame with fear and pain, mingling together to reach a screaming fever pitch inside me. I was not prepared for this. For any of this. Hell, a week ago I was lounging around a beautiful marble palace on the Black Sea coast, not a single care or worry in the world to weigh me down.

Now it feels like the entire earth itself is bearing down on my delicate shoulders, and I don't have the life experience or physical strength to carry it. How was I supposed to know a week ago that my father, the man who has doted on and cared for me my entire life, has been plotting for years to toss me away? He has been grooming and preparing me for a fate I have no say in, like I am some mindless, empty-headed object he can trade off to the highest bidder. I'm nothing but a shiny, pretty asset to him, even though I am his own flesh and blood. The sting of betrayal slinks in underneath the panic and pain, adding another dose of bitterness to the shit cocktail that has become my life. I have spent my whole life comfortable in the role of a spoiled, sheltered little rich girl, and nothing I have done or seen has come even close to preparing me for this moment right now. I can't even believe this is my life: running away from the man who wants to make me his submissive, domestic little wife to dominate and manipulate to his heart's content, all thanks to my father, who I have always trusted to take care of me.

Is he not the man I thought he was? Have I been living a lie all these beautiful years? All the gifts, the lovely clothes, the designer shoes, the makeup, the handbags, the gourmet dining, the trips around the world in first class-- always first class. It's all been a series of coins fed into the vending machine that would pump out the finished product: a demure, pampered, agreeable young woman who does what-ever she is told because she has no reason not to trust.

Me. I'm the finished product. I never saw any of this coming. I never knew what to expect. How could I? At what point in my happy, easy existence was I supposed to notice the malicious evil behind my father's every decision? The motivation for his kindness? The silent, unspoken exchange of power that took place every time he promised me something shiny and new and beautiful?

Right now, I feel like the biggest idiot in the world. And I also feel like I might pass out or fall over at any moment, because my body is not ready for this kind of hasty, dangerous escape. But luckily, my mysterious rescuer seems to have been born for this.

"Come on!" he whispers back at me, glancing over his shoulder.

I can feel tears prickling up in my eyes as my legs start to go numb. I can't tell if we've been running for five minutes or five seconds. Or five years. My mind is so cluttered with panic and adrenaline that it's gone blank. My vision narrows down to a tunnel, to a sharp point. And in the center of what I can still see, what I can still feel, is the powerful man dragging me along dutifully, not abandoning me even though he could move so much faster without me. Holding onto my hand and refusing to let go even though I am just a liability to him. Because whatever the hell he was doing here, hidden in the hedges, I'm not too sheltered to realize it can't have been for a good reason. A *legal* reason.

I wish I could ask him.

What is he doing here? Why is he skulking around Liev Ovechkin's private gardens? Has he been watching me? Is that why I saw him at the airport? The way my father betrayed me has messed with my mind, made me paranoid. I suspect everyone and everything now. Perhaps this man has been watching me all this time. But why?

Right now, it doesn't really matter, though. Because either way, he's helping me now. I may not know his exact intentions and motivations for being here, but I know he can't possibly be any worse than the cruel, ugly, misogynist pig up on the second floor of the mansion. He's saving me from the man I know for a fact is a bad guy. Right now, the why is much less important than the how. As in, how the hell are we going to get out of here? I know Liev well enough to realize that he's got eyes and ears everywhere, just like my father. And guards. There have got be guards around here somewhere. Clearly Liev has realized I'm missing. He knows something is up, and it's only matter of time before--

"Stop!" shouts a loud, deep voice from somewhere off to our left. I gasp with horror as my fear comes true. A guard. But the man pulling me along doesn't listen. He doesn't stop. He doesn't even hesitate for a second. Not even when we burst out of the hedges and into a clearing with a paved walkway, lit with moody bluish tiki torches. Our cover is blown. We're no longer hidden by the greenery. We are totally exposed, and a single quick glance tells me that the guard I heard a moment ago is only about twenty yards away, and he's not empty-handed.

He's holding a gun. A really, really big one. And

he looks like he knows what he's doing with it, too. The guard is dressed in all green camouflage, like some kind of special operations soldier or something. He looks pissed. He starts chasing after us, the barrel of his enormous weapon pointed right at us. I let out a shriek of terror and my savior tightens his grip on my hand, shoving me in front of him so that his body is shielding me, in between the guard and me. Only I don't know where to go. I don't know where to run.

"Weave!" he commands in a low, insistent growl. At first his command makes no sense to me, but he grabs me by the waist, both of his hands on my hips, and guides me first way off to the right, and then back off to the left, so that we're running in a zigzag pattern across the grounds. It occurs to me somewhere in the back of my mind that the whole point is to make us less easy targets, to make the guard have a more difficult time aiming at us. That realization only frightens me more-- I am not used to this level of true danger. I have never had a gun pointed in my direction before.

And my lungs are on fire. I struggle to drag air into my chest as we run so fast, my legs starting to wobble and go weak. My white blouse is stained with sweat and tears and greenish-gray stains from the foliage. The silken sleeves are torn into thin ribbons by the thorns, and I know I must look like a caricature of some desert island castaway right now.

Just then, the pointy heel of my left shoe gets stuck in between two jaunty cobblestones and I nearly stumble to my knees, the sheer momentum of our escape slamming me down. I scream out as the man behind me catches me in his arms for the second time, and the heel of my shoe breaks off, leaving my feet at uneven heights.

I make a split second decision to kick them both off, regaining my composure quickly and breaking into a barefoot, desperate run. My mystery man is hot on my heels, helping me remember to weave. The guard fires a warning shot into the air, and the sound is so loud it makes my ears ring. He's closer now. My momentary stumble set us back a couple of seconds, and in a situation like this, a couple seconds is more than enough to ruin us.

It's over. I can feel it. My body doesn't want to try anymore. I'm so tired.

I look back over my shoulder, wide-eyed, and to my surprise and confusion, the guard isn't there. The blue-eyed man urges me to keep moving, grabbing my hand again and pulling me along behind him. There isn't time to second guess any of it. We just have to move. But I can see the wrought-iron gate ahead of us, looming tall and spiky. And what's more, I notice that on this section of the perimeter, there's barbed wire coiling around the top of the fence.

"Fuck," I hiss to myself. But my mystery guy

doesn't slow down. He seems to have a plan. And as we come closer to the wall, I can squint and make out a dark shape draped over the top of the gate. A jacket. I catch a glint of moonlight reflecting off the shiny coat buttons. And lodged over it is what looks to be… a grappling hook? I grimace at the sight of it, unable to make sense of that in my head. Grappling hooks are the stuff of movies, not real life.

Did this guy seriously use a grappling hook to get over the wall?

There's no time to ask. We run straight up to the wall, and I swivel around to stare at him in confusion. But again, he doesn't hesitate. To my shock, he grabs me by the waist again and hoists me up as easily as if I might be a feather pillow. I don't have time to question it, only to react with pure instinct. I reach out and grab hold of the fence, my hands curling over the thick jacket to protect myself from the barbs. The man steadies my legs with his hands wrapped around my narrow calves and pushes me up so that I can clumsily climb over the top of the fence and drop to the other side. It hurts when I hit the ground, landing on my feet. The impact rattles up through my ankles, and I whimper in pain. A moment later, the man drops down to the ground beside me and helps me up with one strong arm. He all but carries me away through the palm trees and scratchy underbrush. My bare feet sting as I stumble over thorns, and I can tell I'm slowing us down. So without a single word, the man scoops me up over his shoulder and breaks into a sprint, carrying me down the road. In the near total darkness, I can hardly tell which direction we're going, much less what our destination is. But it becomes clear a few seconds alter, when I see the reflection of shiny black finish in the moonlight: a sleek, elegant black car just barely hidden off the side of the road. He yanks open the passenger-side door, cradles me into the seat, and then climbs in behind the steering wheel. He jams the key into the ignition and the engine roars to life. With a high-pitched squeal, the tires roll backward out of the brush and onto the road. He does a quick U-turn and takes off away from Liev's estate, the expensive car rumbling quietly through the peaceful residential neighborhood. I know enough about the area to realize that we've got a long way to go to the interstate. I assume that's where he's headed.

It hits me that I'm in a car with a stranger whose name I don't even know. A man who was lurking in the bushes, who just happened to catch me as I fell. Who is he? What is his intention with me? How did we get here?

I glance over at him in the darkness, my heart still racing. He looks angry, his dark brows furrowed and his jaw tensing up as his hands white-knuckle the wheel. For a split second, I am afraid of him. But then he turns to meet my gaze, and instantly his features soften. He offers me a warm, reassuring smile, just like he did back in the airport, and a feeling of calm floods through my body. I release the long-held breath burning up my lungs. Wherever we're going, it's got to be an improvement upon where I just came from. And whoever he is, I'm grateful to him. I know he knows how bad it was. How desperately I needed to be saved. Regardless of where we end up and regardless of why it's happening, I'm glad he found me.

But my relief is short-lived, because before we even make it out of the ritzy neighborhood, I hear the unmistakable wail of police sirens somewhere in the distance, echoing eerily in the night.

I have dealt with jobs that didn't go according to plan. I've even dealt with jobs that I've had to pull out of at the last minute, jobs that have gone completely haywire and up in flames. But I have never pulled out of a job like this before.

And I have never done it so recklessly.

My livelihood depends on being prepared for every possible situation, but even with the weeks of preparation I put into this hit, I never expected that things could have unfolded in this direction. She should not have been delivered to Liev so quickly, nor could I have ever anticipated that she would do something as brazen as trying to escape with no plan. I can tell that she has only been thinking one step at a time, never knowing what's around the next corner or who might be waiting for her. Had I not been here to save her, there's no telling what would have befallen her.

But she has the good sense to make a move quickly and decisively. That's rare. Most failures in missions like this come from hesitating too long. Who am I to say? This little girl might yet have surprised me.

She has already impressed me.

I hear the sound of her perfectly manicured nails dig into the leather seat as I make my way through the neighborhood. I can tell that she's anxious, not just because of our situation, but because I am not blazing a path through these suburbs so fast that I burn the rubber of my tires.

If I drive too fast and too erratically, someone will report my car to the police. And if they get involved, it's all over. I can dodge the Ovechkin soldiers, but I cannot evade two hunters at once. Not without a firefight that I'm hardly prepared for.

I weave in and out of the winding roads around the stunning manors, staying away from headlights and trying to keep quiet. As I come to a stop at a stop sign, she whips her head over to me, eyes bulging, and I can tell that she's barely holding herself back from asking why the hell we aren't moving. I don't even look at her. I wait a moment at the stop sign, then turn left and carry on my meandering path.

Headlights appear in my rear-view mirror, and I hear the girl suck in a breath. I calmly take a turn right, and I accelerate just enough to take another left further up ahead and loop around a small public park. I move us behind a set of dumpsters and kill the headlights, holding still there until we watch the other black sedan pass us by.

I hear the girl clap a hand to her mouth as we get a glimpse into the car hunting us. The windows are down, and there's a man leaning out of one with a gun in his hand, cruel eyes scanning the area.

I reach over to her, and I put a hand on her knee in silent warning. I can almost hear her heart pounding. She starts to shiver in my hand, and I give her a gentle squeeze. Finally, the car passes, and she allows herself to breathe.

I wait for a full minute before I slowly pull around, following the car that just passed us.

Finally, it seems, she can't hold it back any longer.

"They went this way!" she hisses.

I simply nod, but I say nothing. She stares at me for a long time, and when she finally realizes she isn't getting an answer, she crosses her arms and looks ahead, worrying her lip.

I'm following the other car because they're unlikely to double back. If I went in the opposite direction, there's a good chance I would run into one of the other cars that's undoubtedly also searching for us. Instead, I follow the car at a safe distance for some time before turning off down another road.

The houses all around us are stunning displays of wealth. Each street seems lined with gorgeous tree formations, tall hedges line many of the homes that want to remain private, and there are fabulously expensive cars in every gated driveway. Most of this neighborhood is old money.

I catch a glimpse of her out of the corner of my eye every now and then, and each time it happens, I feel like she electrifies me, like I'm getting a shock of energy each time I dare to look at her. She looks like a wild deer being hunted, from the wild, haunted look in her eyes to her narrow chest rising and falling in short, quick breaths. Her jeans are torn, her hair looks wild, and I feel the urge within me to reach over and smooth it out.

I realize how distracted she is making me. It isn't her fault, of course, but she has an energy around her that I can't explain. She is almost otherworldly in her aura. I have never been so affected by someone in my life. I have rescued people before, but I have never felt like I am pulling an angel out of the jaws of hell.

My car fits in with the luxurious scenery all around this neighborhood, which is good, because nothing will get us caught faster than looking out of place in an area like this. Still, I wind through the neighborhood as carefully as possible. I can still hear the occasional sound of wheels on the road, and it's much later than most respectable people are out at night. I feel like I'm guiding her through shark-infested waters, doing as much work to keep her from knowing just how close to danger we are as actual work avoiding that danger.

More than once, I can sense that we're merely a block away from running into our pursuers, but I stay quiet and calm.

Moreover, she stays quiet too. I like that, not because I don't like the sound of her voice, but because it gives me time to think.

The plan is out the window. Months of plotting and weeks of preparing for this night, all gone up in flames faster than I could blink. It is a setback, but I have long since trained myself not to be affected by such things. Being angry would only lower my already slim chances of surviving this. In my line of work, you can get angry, or you can be successful.

The plan was a very quick and clean hit. I had expected to put a bullet in Ovechkin's head, make my escape, and let none be the wiser. I don't usually carry out hits with a sniper rifle from the bushes-- that's much too close a range than is necessary, and anyone who knows me would know it does not fit my MO. Ideally, nothing would be traced to me. Koroleva would then let his guard down, thinking some rival of Ovechkin's dealt with his biggest enemy, and I would exploit that sense of security to deal with my second man.

Now, I have nothing.

Well, that isn't entirely true.

The scent of the girl's hair reminds me of her every few seconds, a subtle reminder that she's with me, willingly or otherwise. This is an element that I could not have prepared for.

I still don't know what to think of her. She fills my every spare thought, invading my mind like nothing has in a long time, but I've barely spoken a word to her. The way her body is perfectly sculpted with the best resources money can buy tells me a thing or two about her. She lives a life of ease, and the fact that I have barely heard mention of her until recently tells me that Nestor Koroleva keeps her busy out of the picture. My guess is that she has spent most of her life traveling the world, putting carefully-engineered pictures on social media and soaking up an international education.

But everything else? She is a teenage mystery. Such people never get involved in bratva business, and I have nothing to equip me to handle her. I can try to read her mind, but it will do me no good. All I know is that she is desperate, no friend of Liev Ovechkin's. They say the enemy of my enemy is my friend, but I tend to play my cards more cautiously than this.

I feel her eyes on me periodically. She has questions. Dozens of them, I'm sure. But I will not override her and make her my prisoner. One could call her my hostage, but if she wants to draw that conclusion, she can do so herself. The more compliant she is with me, the easier the near future will be, whatever that is.

The fact that she is now bound to me fills me with mixed emotions. On the one hand, it is a risk. Someone like her is not trained to handle this sensitive of a situation. She could be one big liability, a bullet in my head waiting to happen. On the other hand...there is the issue of the effect she has on me. The thought of having her near to me makes my heart pound harder.

I know my body well, and I have been with many women before. I know when I want someone. This girl is beyond forbidden. She is mafia royalty, a princess in her own right. She has lived and breathed a world that I have only watched and preyed upon from the shadows. She is a lamb being abducted by the wolf.

She is the daughter of one of the two men I most want to see dead. We should be enemies. I should use her as a pawn, a resource to be traded off or used as leverage to lure my prey into the open. But all my body wants is to claim her for myself.

The way she looks at me tells me volumes about her thoughts, too. Silence is often more honest than conversation.

But at last, she breaks the silence of the drive.

"Are you with them?"

I arch an eyebrow at her, glancing at her briefly.

"I saw you at the airport. At JFK," she says. There is nervousness in her voice, but she does a decent job of channeling it into boldness. "When I arrived in the States, I saw you there, in the shadows. You were watching me. Are you with them?"

There's more force behind the question a second time. Her fear is catching up to her, and she wants to know just who she's dealing with.

"You're an important woman," I say simply. "There were probably many people at the airport. What makes you sure you saw me?"

"Your eyes," she says without missing a beat. "I could recognize them under the ski mask earlier."

I am mildly surprised by that. She has a sharp attention to detail, it seems. Still, I show no reaction. Another silence falls between us, but her eyes never leave me. I feel her scrutinizing me, searching for more. She is hungry for knowledge, and I know this girl isn't going to let secrets lie easily.

"No," she finally says, "you're not with my dad's people. You wouldn't have disappeared when you did. I keep track of the handlers my dad assigns me better than he thinks."

Now, I am more than mildly surprised. This is not the spoiled, wilting flower of a mafia princess I was expecting. Or if she is, she is a particularly astute one.

"You're not with the police, either," she says, and I can't help but crack a smile. "I've seen how deep some sting operations can be, I know it's not impossible."

"Who, then?" I ask.

She is silent for a long pause, glaring hard at me.

"This isn't a game," she finally says.

"I am with nobody," I say, and it's the most honest I've been with anyone in a long time.

"Oh," she replies.

Of all the possible answers to that statement, I wasn't expecting one so simple. I have to fight the urge to let out a chuckle. I have to wonder what the life of a mafia princess like her is like. Being a pawn of the bratva bosses like Nestor and Liev is one thing. Your life is always on the line, and bosses like them never care, not truly. Only in my line of work can a man have some independence in how he handles things, and even then, my relationship with them is brittle on the best of days, no matter how warm the smiles and the handshakes are.

But a girl like her never feels such freedom, even less than the men who work for them. This girl is both the resource and a source of pride for Nestor-- a liability and an asset all in one. She is someone to spoil and someone to worry over. She has been pulled around like this her whole life, and I realize that she must be more aware of how strong her leash truly is than I ever expected.

I might not even be the first person to abduct her.

"Why were you down there?" she asks.

I say nothing. I let my eyes go to her, and I make eye contact that says a hundred words. She can figure that out, if she really wants to know.

Another long silence.

"Do you know who I am?" she asks.

"I do, Anastasia," I say.

"Where are you taking me?" she finally asks, an uneasy edge to her voice.

"Somewhere safe," I say.

"Am I safe with you?" she asks. The question sends a shiver through my body of desire mixed with intrigue. The way she puts her questions is strange. She seems to be angling for something that I can't put my finger on.

"We'll see," I say, and I watch her manicured hands squeeze the seat again.

The drive takes us close to the highway, our ticket out of here. I can see the exit up ahead, and I maintain a steady speed, drawing a deep breath.

And just a hundred yards from the exit, my eyes snap up to the rear-view mirror.

Blue and red lights flash behind us.

Anastasia gasps, turning her head and then looking to me with a wild look in her eyes.

I clench my jaw. So close.

But there's nobody else on the road, not a chance in the world that the officer could be pulling anyone else over. The cruiser gets closer to us, and I realize there's no way out of this.

"What are you doing?!" Anastasia blurts as I put on the brakes and slowly bring the car to the side of the road.

Time to do some acting.

Terror and panic floods through my body just like it did before. I was foolish to think I might be safe with this man. But as terrified as I am, he seems equally calm. A placid, easy smile warms his features and he gives me a wink. I frown at him.

"Are you insane? While are you so okay with this?" I hiss frantically.

He snakes his large hand across the center console and grabs my hand, giving it a squeeze. Then he shrugs, shaking his shoulders as though he's an athlete loosening up his muscles before a big hurdle. Like he's getting into character. Yeah. He must be crazy.

"What are we going to do?" I ask, turning in my seat to stare at the bright flashing lights of the police car. I can just barely make out the figure of the cop behind the wheel as the squad car squeaks to a stop behind us. The lights don't cut out, even as the siren goes silent.

"We're going to play it cool," says my escort, smiling beatifically.

"Play it cool?" I repeat, eyes going wide. My mouth falls open as I splutter for a response. "Wh-what the hell do you mean? How can we possibly play it cool? There's a damn police officer coming to arrest us. Or you. Or me. Probably both of us."

"Anastasia," he says. But I can't stop rambling, my thoughts are so tangled up.

"Oh my god. I can't go to jail. I-I won't survive. I don't even like sharing a bathroom with a friend. What if they put me in solitary confinement? With no phone? No Internet? Oh god. And I'm not a fighter. I don't know how to throw a punch. I'm going to get my ass kicked," I whisper.

"Anastasia," he says again, ineffectually.

"Maybe not jail. Maybe the cop will just drag me back home to my father so he can kick my ass instead. Or worse-- he'll take me back to Uncle Liev and let him deal with me. Oh no. I can't face that. My father's going to be so angry and whatever Uncle Liev does with me will be a million times worse than anything that could happen in prison," I whimper, tears burning in my eyes as I begin to tremble.

"Ana," says the mystery guy, more emphatically this time. He gives my hand a quick little shake to get my attention, then slowly raises it to his lips. Without breaking eye contact with me at all, he lightly kisses my fingers and smiles.

"What are you doing?" I murmur. A tingling warmth is radiating through my entire body from his gentle touch. No one has ever touched me this way before, not even the boys I've dated off and on throughout the years. I have never let any of them get close enough. Nowhere close. But somehow, nonsensically, despite all the craziness and danger of the predicament we are currently neck-deep in, the way he touches me feels… natural. It feels right. In a way that nothing ever has before.

"Here's the story," he says calmly. "You and I are newlyweds."

"What?" I hiss, tilting my head to one side.

"Just listen," he tells me. "We're newlyweds taking a night drive. We were supposed to have a big lavish wedding with all our friends and family but we got impatient. Decided the hundred-thousand-dollar wedding on a Caribbean beach just wasn't for us. So we eloped, just the two of us and a witness down at the courthouse. And now we're making a getaway, riding off in the middle of the night to go to our honeymoon."

"Wow," I mutter, shaking my head. "You really thought of all this right now? On the spot?" He smiles at me and winks again.

"Yes. Everything is going to be fine. Just play

along," he instructs me. My heart skips a beat when I hear the faint clacking of the cop's shoes on the pavement. He's out of the squad car now, coming our way, with his hands at his belt. Is he reaching for a gun? I'm too afraid to look and find out.

"Wait-- what if he asks for our ID? What if he asks our names?" I insist.

"Well, my name is Nikolai. And yours is Anastasia," he says matter-of-factly.

"Nikolai? Really?" I ask, squinting at him. "Is that your fake name for the purposes of the massive lie we're about to tell, or--"

"It's my real name. Nice to meet you," Nikolai says, smooth as velvet.

"Oh. Um. Nice to meet you, too. Thanks for saving my life. But how the hell are we going to survive this? I've never even been pulled over before. I-I don't know what to do," I admit, blushing.

"Doesn't matter. Just leave the talking to me. And don't forget to smile. Look happy. Remember, we're on the way to our honeymoon," he says.

"Oh my god," I breathe, closing my eyes and willing my heart to slow down from its rollicking pace as the cop saunters up to the car and bends down slightly to peer in the window. The mystery guy rolls down the window, cool as a cucumber, even though I'm doing my best not to even make eye contact with the cop. I'm worried that if he sees my eyes, he will be able to somehow read my mind and know we're lying.

"Good evening, officer," greets Nikolai, holding out his hand for the cop to shake. The police officer gawks at it in confusion for a moment, clearly unaccustomed to his potential perpetrators greeting him with such affability.

"Good evening, sir," the cop replies. "How are you doing tonight?"

Nikolai chuckles and shakes his head, somehow making it look convincing. "Well, I have to be honest with you, officer-- I'm in one hell of a great mood," he begins brightly. It takes all my strength not to gasp or whimper. What the hell is he doing? He squeezes my hand.

"Oh. Is that so?" the officer inquires, frowning slightly. "And why is that?"

Nikolai holds up the hand that's gripping mine and grins from ear to ear. "Because tonight, my wife and I are headed off to our honeymoon. I've never been happier," he declares.

The cop looks mildly amused. "Your honeymoon? Really? In the middle of the night?"

Oh god. He knows we're lying. But Nikolai doesn't flinch. "Well, you see, we eloped in secret," he explains, lowering his voice to a conspiratorial tone.

"Eloped?" repeats the cop, folding his arms over his chest and widening his stance.

"Yes, sir. See, my wife and I were supposed to

have this big, lavish wedding. Really over the top. The budget was going to be just totally crazy. I mean, her mother was talking about flying in a full orchestra from Germany to play the wedding march, imported lavender from the south of France, a wedding cake with twenty tiers-- the works. We're talking a hundred-thousand dollars blown on one big night," Nikolai explains.

"Uh-huh. Wow," says the cop. Oh my god. Is he… starting to believe our cover story?

"And I mean, don't get me wrong, if that's what my sweetheart wanted, I would've written off that check like it was nothing. I love my little angel, and she can have whatever she wants. But we started talking and realized, you know what?"

"What?" asks the cop, smiling now.

Nikolai gives him an exaggerated shrug. "We don't need all that! After all, our marriage isn't about money or fancy orchestras or any of that shallow, superficial stuff. It's about love. And love doesn't have to cost a damn thing."

"That's real nice," the cop admits. Holy shit. He's buying it. He's drinking our Koolaid.

"I agree," chuckles Nikolai. He glances over at me with a twinkle in his eye. A genuine twinkle. He lets go of my hand and lets his fingers roam up my thigh, gripping me softly. Again, that warm and tingly twinge passes over my body and I have to remind myself to breathe.

"So, anyway, we went down to the courthouse and decided to just get the paperwork done there. Found a random witness, made up our vows right on the spot, and got hitched. You're looking at a brand new pair of married lovers! Husband and wife, can you believe it?" Nikolai exclaims, still grinning. His smile is infectious. The cop smirks, nodding at us.

"That's a beautiful story. Congratulations, you two," he says. "But why are you leaving in the middle of the night?"

"Oh," I cut in suddenly. "Well, to be perfectly honest with you, my mother is the one who wanted the big wedding in the first place. She had her heart set on it. So when she finds out we eloped, she's going to be… disappointed, to say the least. We want to get out of town and head off to our honeymoon before she finds out. We've got a cabin up in Montauk where we're going to spend the weekend, just the two of us. Don't worry, I plan on giving Mom a call before we disappear. But for right now, it's just better if she doesn't know."

Nikolai looks impressed with my ability to lie. The cop nods slowly, taking it all in.

"Well, I suppose that makes sense. But don't you forget to call her. My mother would kill me if I pulled something like that," jokes the police officer. Nikolai and I both force a laugh. The cop looks pleased. "Alright, folks. Hang tight for a moment. Let me go check with something in my squad car. I'll be back in just a minute. Don't worry. I won't keep you waiting long."

"Sure, sure," Nikolai replies good-naturedly. The cop stalks back to his car and Nikolai rolls the window up, then turns to me. "Good work," he says.

"Thanks," I answer quickly. "But what the hell do we do now? He never said why he pulled us over. What if he runs the plate and finds out you're lying?"

Nikolai's hand is still on my thigh, and his fingers have found a patch where the denim is torn from the hedges earlier. He strokes the bare skin there and I shiver, feeling a new, strange sensation between my legs. My eyes widen, and he smiles. "Everything is fine," he says softly.

I can't deny that I love the way it feels-- his hand on my thigh. It's such a warm, intimate gesture that suddenly I can't keep my feelings bottled up anymore. He makes me feel vulnerable and strong at the same time, and I need to get this all out.

"Nikolai, I'm scared," I confess. "Uncle Liev-- Mr. Ovechkin-- is not a good man. I-I can't explain how I know that, but I do. He's been in my life for years, since I was a little girl, and I was too naive to realize it then, but I think he's some kind of crim-inal or something. But not just any run-of-the-mill bad guy; he's powerful, Nikolai. He's got so much money and influence. He owns a lot of stuff. A lot of people. What if he owns the police, too? What if they're, you know, in his pocket or whatever they say?"

Nikolai nods calmly, listening to my fears without reducing them or making me feel silly for it. Then he squeezes my thigh gently and my fear melts into lust instantly for a moment. I wonder if he knows just how much of an effect he's having on me. How can he *not* know?

"I know a lot about Liev Ovechkin," he growls darkly. "I know precisely what kind of a man he is, and you're right in your suspicions. He is not someone you want to mess with."

"Oh god. What do we do? He's going to find us. Maybe that cop is calling to tell him where we are right now!" I whisper fiercely. But his hand just wanders higher and higher up my thigh, making my breath hitch in my throat. Nikolai gives me a slow, knowing smile. My heart skips a beat.

"I can handle it. Whatever happens, I will take care of it. And I will take care of you," he promises me, those bright blue eyes piercing into my very soul.

The cop comes strolling back over, and Nikolai turns to face him with a smile, same as before. "So, officer, what's the damage?" he asks cheerily.

"Well, nothing too serious, sir. I can see why you'd be in a hurry, but you still need to be careful, alright? And this is a nice neighborhood, quiet at night. You might want to slow down and make sure those brights are on. I know you're trying to make a sneaky getaway, but you don't want to sneak up on some other motorist without your brights on and cause a collision, do you? I mean, that would slow you down a whole lot more than your mother-in-law would," the cop guffaws, clearly proud of his own joke.

Nikolai forces a laugh, and I'm impressed at how natural it sounds. "Sure, sure. That makes perfect sense, officer. You got it," he says jovially.

"Okay, then. I'm going to let you off with just a warning, but you be more cautious from here on out, you hear?" the cop insists.

"Of course, sir. You're right. We don't want to cause an accident. Do we, sweetheart?" Nikolai asks, glancing at me. I hurriedly force my lips to shape into some semblance of a smile and nod vigorously.

"Yep. You're right. Yes, sir. We'll be more c-careful," I reply.

"Alrighty, then. You two lovebirds have a nice night. And congratulations again on the nuptials," says the cop.

"Thank you!" Nikolai and I both quip at the same time. The cop gives us an awkward little salute and heads back to his car. Nikolai calmly rolls up the window, turns on the engine, and starts to slowly pull away onto the road again. I'm wracked with emotion. Fear, relief, elation, confusion, amazement-- and lust. He handled that so well, so calmly. He's perfectly in control, making me feel safe with him. I know I can trust Nikolai. He said he would take care of me, and I find myself believing him.

As we drive away, Nikolai's hand is still on my thigh, making its way up slowly. And I like it. I don't know what kind of magical hold he has over me, but my fear is turning into adrenaline, and it's a different kind of rush than what I felt before. It's more primal. Warmer. More intoxicating, and in a good way. I find myself wanting to rip off my clothes and his. Suddenly, the danger of our predicament feels less like a bear trap waiting to snatch us up and more like, well, a thrill. We make it only a little bit farther down the road, though, before some fresh panic attacks us: the engine, previously purring smoothly, suddenly cuts out.

NIKOLAI

"What happened?" Ana says as I guide the car to a slow stop on the side of the road. Thankfully, nobody else is on this particular road, giving me free rein to pull over at a convenient spot. "Are we out of gas?"

"No," I say, peering at the blank dashboard. "The engine died."

"What?!" she blurts, starting to look more panicked. "How? This car looks, like, ridiculously nice, doesn't it have failsafes of some kind?"

I crack a smile, raising my eyebrows at her. "Ever hear the saying, 'they don't make them like they used to'?"

She tightens her jaw as I pop the hood and step out of the car. Circling around to the front, I see no smoke or flames, so that's one plus. I start checking the usual culprits of a stalled engine, but it doesn't take long for Ana to open the door and step out, creeping around to the front of the car with me.

"Are you a mechanic, too? Is that part of your cover story?" she asks, and there's a playful smile on her face. To say I'm surprised by her candor in a situation like this is an understatement, but not an unwelcome surprise.

"No," I admit, "but you don't grow up in Russia without learning your way around a car, no matter who you are. If your vehicle breaks down on a forest backroad in the middle of a Russian winter, you'd better know how to get it running again. Or you'll be running for your life."

She hovers around me, craning her neck to look at what I'm doing, and she occasionally glances back and forth down the long, black road.

"Should...should we be worried about them? The guys from the mansion, I mean."

"No," I say a third time. "There are many different directions we could have taken out of the neighborhood, and this is one I planned ahead of time and cased for several nights. They don't check down this road, and we're already a long way away."

She nods, swallowing, but she looks vaguely reassured by my words.

"What do you think is wrong with it?" she asks.

"Faulty fuel injector," I grunt, standing up from the hood and wiping my hands on my pants, frowning. "I was hoping for just a dead battery, but this isn't something that is easy to fix on the roadside."

"Shit," she murmurs as I pull out my phone to start thumbing through an app, furrowing my eyebrows. "Okay, so...any ideas on what to do?" She gets a wry smile on her face, sarcastically suggesting, "I don't suppose they have some kind of roadside assistance for tense, borderline-illegal road trips?"

"That's exactly what I'm calling in," I say as I finish filling out the short request for roadside assistance, and Ana's jaw drops.

"Are...are you serious?"

"Unless you like the idea of hiking the rest of the way to where I was taking you," I say mildly, sitting on the hood of the car after I shut it, "then yes, I am."

She stares at me for a few moments in disbelief, then gives her head a little shake. "I can't believe this. What kind of rescue involves a tow?"

"The kind that was never meant to be a rescue in the first place," I say with a challenging smile. "I had a very different plan for how the night was going to unfold before you decided to test your skills climbing out of a window."

Her face turns pink, but she knows she can't argue that.

"Besides," I say, crossing my arms, "this is no rescue, remember? We're just a young couple out for a drive on this lovely night."

She smirks, and she takes slow, meandering steps

toward me, smoothing her clothes out as she avoids my gaze for a few moments before speaking again.

"Well, what *was* the plan for tonight, before things...changed?" she asks, measuring the last word carefully.

I stand up from the car, taking a few steps directly toward her, and she freezes in place on the road. This is the first time that we've stood face to face without being about to run for our lives, and it's the first time that she has has to look up at me like this. The sight of her small frame contrasted with my tall, broad one makes her still. She bites her lip as I peer down at her thoughtfully.

"Take my young lover somewhere nice and private, of course," I say in a low tone. "Somewhere quiet, preferably," I add. "The traffic tonight has left something to be desired."

She can't help but smile at that, but even she can sense how ridiculous this all is. She very literally fell into my arms barely an hour ago, yet we've been working together as well as if we've been working together for years. She catches on quickly and acts skillfully. I can't say the same of some supposedly seasoned veterans I've worked with in the past.

And the energy that has been crackling between us the entire time has been harder and harder to ignore--for both of us.

"I think that doesn't sound half bad," she says.

A shadow of a smile crosses my lips just before

my phone buzzes. I glance down at it and see that I have a text from roadside assistance. My smile turns back into a frown.

"ETA: two hours," I say. Damn. This is the time of night drunks get into accidents, so it should be no surprise that we'll have a wait before we get picked up. But her face falls, and she looks worried.

"Do you think they'll catch up to us?" she asks. "That's a long time to be sitting ducks."

"It is," I admit, "but of all the things they could expect from an escape like ours, breaking down on the side of a road is not one of them. They won't even be looking down these roads, much less watching for a broken-down car."

"I guess we have some time, then," she says. I arch an eyebrow at her, and I see a little pink come to her cheeks, as if she wasn't even sure where she was going with that comment. This girl is getting more intriguing by the moment.

Adrenaline is still running through our veins. It's a strange feeling, but I've felt it enough to give it some thought. It's like a primal, unstoppable force urging you to do *something*, anything to get all that energy out. It makes your senses so much higher and your reflexes quicker that standing still and waiting is the absolute last thing you want. In other words, it's the most agitating feeling imaginable for this exact situation.

I have felt it enough to know how to restrain it.

But for Anastasia, this is her first time feeling that rush. I can see it in her eyes. There's a spark to her that she's almost afraid of, but in the rush of everything, staying still is the worst fate imaginable. Her mind has to stay moving if her body doesn't, and it can wander to places she never thought she could go.

After an uncomfortably long silence, she opens the back door and takes a seat, with her legs sticking out the front as she looks up at me.

"Thank you, by the way," she says. "I don't know why you did what you did, or whether I'm even safe now, but...whatever's going on, it's better than being back there."

"How can you be so sure about that?" I say, putting a hand on the open door and looming over her. She gives me a nervous smile.

"Now, that's not the most reassuring my rescuer can say," she says, but the excitement in her voice is so thick I can taste it in the air. She's frightened and excited all in one, and she is the kind of person to keep pushing that as much as she can.

"Always be ready for anything in the future," I say.

"You told me you were taking me somewhere safe," she says.

"And we're not there yet," I say. "But tell me, Anastasia, do you feel safe with me?"

She stares up at me for a few tense moments, then swallows. "I...I don't know. I want to."

"How do you decide whether to trust a man?" I ask, narrowing my eyes.

"I trust my instincts."

I put my foot on the bottom of the car and bend over, halfway inside the car, just a few inches away from her face as she blushes. I look long and hard into those eyes, those storms of feelings that want so desperately for her to get a hold of herself.

"What do your instincts tell you?" I ask in a low, husky tone.

"That I'm in danger," she whispers. As she does, I feel a small, warm hand on my thigh. I put my hand over it and give it a squeeze.

"You should listen to your instincts better," I growl, and without a second thought, I wrap my hand around the back of her head, fingers through her hair, and I draw her into a deep kiss.

Her whole body tenses up at first as I lean into the car, slowly lowering her onto her back in the back seat. I let go of the outside and enter, kneeling over her as our lips press into each other, and the sound of her sharp, surprised gasp is sweeter than an angel plucking a harp. At first, she doesn't know what to do. She is young, frightened, and desperate for attention. Her body is warm, and her face gets warmer the longer the kiss goes on.

Finally, I bring my lips away. I see her face--eyes

closed, mouth hanging open, then a sudden look of worry on her face, asking me silently why I stopped.

"And what do they say now?" I ask.

"That you just took me for yourself," she whispers.

"Would you like that?"

"I just want to forget, for one night," she answers, and one of her hands touches my chest, grasping me, pulling me.

It's all the invitation I need.

This is wrong in many, many ways. This was supposed to be an assassination, and it has turned into not only a rescue, but a near-kidnapping. The girl in my hands is inexperienced. I can feel it in her every nervous movement. But those eyes have drawn me in from the moment I saw her, and neither of us want to hold back those feelings anymore.

I am a cautious man. The risks I take are measured, and when I act, I am deadly. But now, in this empty road with nothing but the stars and two personalities that seem to click against all odds, in the heat of being hunted, it feels like all those restraints are gone. In some way, this is the world she lives in, but only ever under her father's steady hand.

Now, she is in mine.

I kiss her, but this time, her body turns to electricity around me. Her hands search my muscles, feeling the hardness of my body as I grasp her behind her neck and on her hips, feeling her with a strong, aggressive grip. I guide her down, pushing her hands where I know she wants to feel me. I make her feel the abs running down my stomach to the V that points to my crotch. I let her feel my thighs that seem chiseled from marble. I tease her hair, coaxing her to be bolder with her tongue as our mouths open to each other.

Her sighs are like music, and our motions in the cramped back of the car are like a dance. She is cautious, but I bring her out of her shell. I give her silent cues with my hands, and she feels around me, desperate for more with every passing second. This girl is starved, I can tell. She isn't just inexperienced, she's a virgin.

I stole a virgin mafia princess from one of the most powerful men in New York City, only to sin with her in the middle of nowhere that very night. But it's so much more than that. For her part, she is fleeing the marriage arranged by that same man and her own father. This is teenage rebellion, and I feel like the devil himself.

That isn't a new feeling for me.

I have come to enjoy it.

My hips grind against her, and she can feel my thick shaft through my pants against her thighs. She whimpers when she realizes how large my manhood is, but she gets that much more excited. I break away from her mouth to loom over her and gaze into her face as I feel up her breasts. My large, strong hands are gentle at first, teasing around her shirt, feeling their shape. The feel of this intoxicating woman is everything I imagined and more, and I cannot deny that I imagined her. My body is full of need, and I'm going to let it loose on her.

Her pants are torn, so it will be that much easier to get them down. I bring my hand to the waist and run my thumb around it, teasing at what I want. She slows down, and I look into wide eyes that gleam with desire.

"I…" she starts, "I've never…"

"I know," I say. "I will show you something first."

She grips the seat and breathes slowly and carefully as I work her pants down her hips. She wiggles to help herself out of them, and I bring her underwear with the pants to reveal her untouched lower lips. I let out a rumble of hunger from my chest as my fiendish eyes glower at them. I look back up to meet her gaze, and I stick two fingers into my mouth, getting them wet before I slide them down to her lower lips without further warning.

She gasps as I make small, slow circles and feel how swollen her clit is. Her face is a beautiful mess of color, and I can't help but smile at her. She starts to push her hips up into me, but my hands are firm and steady. I put a hand on her hip and hold her down, subjecting her to relentless torment as I touch her. She is already wet, and she just gets wetter the more I tease her. When I take my hand away, she whimpers in need and protest, but her face goes cherry-red when I bring my fingers to my lips again and taste her honey.

"I want more," I say. As I do, my hands go to her thighs and start to part them with a steady, unstoppable force. A shiver goes up her whole body, so strong that I can feel it and share in its delight.

My face has stubble on it. I bring it to her inner thigh and let out a slow, hot breath as I brush up against it, feeling how soft and ripe she is. My face trails all the way down to where her legs meet, and she lets out a groan of desire at the feeling.

"Has anyone touched you like this, Anastasia?" I ask.

"No," she breathes. "I've wanted it so badly, but it's only ever been in my imagination. All of this feels so..."

"Unreal?" I say. "Adrenaline will do that to you."

"I don't want to waste a second," she purrs. I feel fire flare up in my chest, and I dive in.

My tongue rolls over her lips, licking away the honey already there, and she gasps in pure lust. Her hips try to buck up into my face to feel more of my touch, but my grip on her hips is strong. She whimpers and moans in protest as I hold her down, just teasing the surface of her lips with every stroke.

"Please," she complains.

"Spoiled brat," I growl, "how does it feel to be denied something?"

"Fuck you," she moans.

"Strong words, after what you just saw me do," I say. "Are you always so brazen?"

In response, she reaches up to my head and holds onto it, fingers in my hair, nails digging into my scalp. I chuckle, satisfied.

I reward her with a little more.

My tongue dives into her, and I taste her wet, needy pussy. She's overflowing with honey, and she lets out a delighted sigh when I finally touch those parts of her she wanted dearly. My tongue wanders down into her, then up to her clit from there, which I give the slightest of touches before going back down again.

I lick her pussy over and over again like that, making a mess of her and my face as I tease more honey from her. Her hips never stop trying to push up, trying to get any control back from me, and even her hands try to get me further down on her pussy, but I know what I want, and I'm going to both get it and give it to her.

I get into a steady rhythm, but each time, I tease a little more of her clit. I never give it the attention it really needs, because I want to push her to her limits.

Her skin is perfect. I've never tasted or touched anything like it, and I've had women all over the world. My instincts were right when I first laid eyes on her, and by the way she writhes in my grasp, I can tell hers were as well.

After what feels like an eternity, I start letting my tongue wash over her clit. The first time I touch all of it, she lets out a sharp whimper, and I feel sharp nails on my scalp that delights me. My heavy heart pounds in my musclebound chest, and my whole body works to please her. There is no feeling in the world like this, adrenaline or no.

My tongue darts out, striking her clit with deadly precision each time. I let it linger a little longer with every stroke, teasing just enough that she feels like something is barely out of reach.

Then I feel a change in her. It's subtle, but it's there. Her body starts to tense, and her sighs and moans get more strained. I start getting faster with every stroke, lavishing her with attention and holding nothing back from her. This is the moment to let it all out, and I want to deny this princess nothing in this very moment.

Finally, her mouth falls open, her face blushes, and I feel a flood of honey coat my lips as she comes. Her voice cracks, but she lets out a long, high-pitched groan of ecstasy as her whole body convulses with the force of the orgasm. It pulses through her with her heart, and it goes on so long that I get lost in her wet folds.

I have to have her. I need to enter her. And I will.

When the orgasm finally dies down, I pull my

face from her, looking at her with pure hunger and desire, and I wipe the honey from my face and smile.

My hands go to my pans, cock threatening to burst out if I don't set it free soon.

The next moment, I freeze.

Out of the corner of my eye, I catch something reflected in the rear-view mirror.

My jaw clenches at what I see.

Blue and red lights are approaching again.

That fucking cop.

My chest is heaving, every inch of my body positively on fire with the overwhelming waves of pleasure undulating from my head to my toes, all centered around the sweet spot between my thighs. I can feel my pussy aching, dripping honey down my thighs to dampen the cushy leather seat underneath me. My fingers grip the sides of the seat, one of my arms hooked around the head rest as I breathe deeply and erratically. I have never known a sensation like this before. Nothing the incredible rush, the release of so much tension held in my every muscle. I have only ever even touched myself a few times in my life, and I never got very much out of it. In fact, it has always been so unsatisfying that I found myself pretty much completely uninterested in sex-- after all, if I couldn't make myself feel good, what hope would anyone else have of satisfying me? I assumed maybe I was broken. Faulty. Built incorrectly. Or maybe all my girl friends back in school who ranted and raved about the joys of dry-humping their boring milque-toast boyfriends in secret hiding places on the school grounds were just lying to me. Or at the very least, exaggerating the experiences.

But now? My mind is both blown and changed. Sex can feel good, when you're with someone who knows what he's doing. It's like Nikolai can read my mind, like his fingers and his tongue can sense what my body aches for even before I know the answer myself. Perhaps this is reckless. Maybe it's stupid to be half-undressed in the back seat of some strange man's car after very narrowly escaping the predatory clutches of the man I am supposed to marry. But right now? I don't care. I feel way too good to give a damn what happens to us. Between the rush of adrenaline and the dopamine flowing through my body, courtesy of Nikolai's expert lips and tongue, I feel exhilarated. Free. I have seen the light.

But then I see a different light, reflected in the rear view mirror upfront. Not only that, but Nikolai has suddenly stopped doing that magical thing he does with his tongue. I look down at him, confused and disoriented by the thrill of pleasure still coursing up and down my body, and I'm surprised to see the look of concern on his face. Those thick, black eyebrows are knitting together in the middle, his jaw tensing up. He wipes his mouth and sighs.

"*Der'mo*," he murmurs, hurriedly snatching up my jeans and thrusting them at me.

"What does that mean?" I ask. I'm getting worried now. Why did he stop?

"It means shit," Nikolai answers quickly. "Put your jeans back on, and hurry. That damn cop is back."

"What?" I burst out, my eyes going wide with terror. My hands start trembling, which only makes it more difficult to yank my jeans back on over my legs. They're from a designer brand, so of course they're made without a single ounce of stretch to them, and it's difficult to put them on without standing and jumping up and down.

"Stay calm, but move fast," he warns me as he clambers back into the front seat, somehow making it look smooth and effortless even though he's got to be several inches over six feet and broad as a grizzly bear. He slides behind the wheel and rakes his fingers back through his dark hair, breathing slowly and closing his eyes to calm down and get back into character. I wonder if it's going to be the same exact cop as before. What are the odds?

I finally manage to get my jeans on as the flashing blue and red lights behind us get brighter and brighter. Then I hear the telltale squeal of the squad car brakes and I all but leap into the passenger seat, desperately trying to smooth down my wild hair and make myself look presentable. Like Nikolai hasn't just rocked my world and left me reeling.

"Stay calm," he assures me. "Everything will be okay. I'm pretty certain that's the same cop. Either way, we stick to our story, alright?"

I nod nervously, biting my lip. "Okay. Okay. Yeah. We got this," I mutter, not convincing either of us, most especially myself. But Nikolai turns and smiles softly at me and reaches over to pat my thigh, sending another thrill of delight through my core, despite the fear bumping my heartbeat up.

"Wh-what should we tell him?" I hiss, turning in my seat to look back at the cop.

"Don't look," he commands. I hurriedly turn back around and start fidgeting with a lock of hair tangled over my shoulder.

"Nikolai, I'm scared. Surely he's going to know something's up this time," I admit.

"No, we're just two newlyweds in trouble. We need to get to our honeymoon, but our car broke down. We won't be in trouble. We'll be the ones needing help, not getting arrested," he tells me earnestly. "We don't look like trouble. We look normal."

I snort, rolling my eyes. "Yeah, there's nothing normal about any of this."

Nikolai nods slowly, staring off down the road as we both hear the cop's footsteps approaching for the second time. "You're right about that, Ana," he replies quietly.

He rolls the window down and plasters that same goofy, innocuous-looking grin on his handsome face again, leaning an arm out the window as the cop steps up and bends down, just like he did before. This is deja vu in the worst possible way.

"Now, folks, when you said you were on the way to your honeymoon, I thought you were at least going to make it out of town," jokes the cop, smiling broadly. Oh, that's a good start.

Nikolai groans and shrugs. "What can you do? These flashy new cars are all looks and no muscle. What's the use of having something shiny and new if it can't even get you from point A to point B?" he says good-naturedly. The cop chuckles.

"You kids alright in there?" he asks, squinting as he peers around Nikolai to look at me. I can feel his eyes taking in my disheveled, off-kilter appearance. He quirks an eyebrow, trying not to be smug about the inference he's making here. I give him a sheepish smile and reflexively reach up to try and smooth my messy hair down.

"We, uh, tried to make the best of a bad situation, if you know what I mean," Nikolai confesses to the cop. My jaw drops. He's really throwing us under the bus! I wonder to myself if it really is illegal to have sex in a parked car in a private neighborhood. What crime would that be? Disturbing the peace? Public indecency? All the most worrying thoughts go through my mind at the same time. But the cop seems surprisingly nonplussed by the situation.

"Ah, to be young and in love again," the officer muses. "Why, you two are just like high schoolers parked at makeout creek, aren't you?"

Nikolai forces a laugh. "Yeah. You caught us. But when your car breaks down en route to your honeymoon, what else can you do? We called roadside assistance but they won't be here for hours, so one thing led to another and..." he trails off.

"Fair enough," guffaws the cop. "But the truth is, I can't have the two of you necking on the side of the road. What if some late-night jogger comes by and sees something... untoward? So let me offer you something: I can get you a tow. I don't know how far away your honeymoon cabin is, but there's this cute little small town just a while down the road called Roslyn. I should know-- it's where I live, actually. Anyway, there's this adorable bed and breakfast where you could rent a little cottage out back. It's a mother-in-law suite, but it's well-furnished and private and, well, I could rave about it forever, but I'm sure you'd rather just go ahead and get there."

I blink in surprise at how easily the cop bought our story hook, line, and sinker. He's even going out of his way to help us find a "honeymoon" spot for the night. Either this is the world's most helpful government employee, or Nikolai is the most convincing actor in the universe. Or, I reason, it's probably both. Nikolai taps the steering wheel, grinning at the cop.

"Wow, that is a fantastic idea, officer," he says brightly. "We would love that, wouldn't we, honey?" he asks, turning to me and giving me an emphatic nod.

I nod. "Yes. Yep. That's a great idea. Perfect. Let's do that," I say awkwardly.

The cop claps his hands together. "Great! It's a plan. I can have my tow guy here in just a few minutes, no worries."

He stalks off to make a call, while Nikolai and I exchange amused expressions. The cop's word is good. Within ten minutes, there's a tow truck and a police escort taking us to the cute little town of Roslyn. And the cop wasn't lying about the mother-in-law suite, either. Even though it's damn near midnight, the owner of the bed and breakfast, who is a little old lady with horn-rimmed glasses, lets us check in without so much as a complaint. With the car at a mechanic down the street, the cop bids us goodnight and congratulates us again on our fake marriage before heading back out on patrol. Nikolai and I settle into our quaint little cottage, the windows pleasantly shrouded by flowering trees and bushes. The place looks like it was decorated by a high-society lady from the 1800s, but it's cozy, and it's far better than being stuck on the side of the road barely ten miles from Ovechkin's mansion.

Once we're locked into the cottage, we both heave a sigh of relief.

"Did that really just happen?" I ask, still dumbfounded by our stroke of good luck.

Nikolai nods. "Seems that way. Yes. Let's not overthink it."

I glance at the antique grandfather clock across the room, squinting to read the time. It's nearly two in the morning. I groan. "I haven't stayed up this late since the last day at my finishing school when my dorm mates and I had a sleepover and drank cheap wine all night," I admit, smiling at the memory. Then I frown, as the reality of how much things have changed in just over a week hits me straight in the face.

"What's wrong?" Nikolai asks, standing up and walking over to sit next to me on the edge of the floral-print chaise lounge. I stare down at my bare feet, overcome with emotion.

"It's just that… my life seems to be going totally off the rails. I mean, my lifestyle has always been a little abnormal, what with all the traveling and the designer clothes and the-- well, everything that comes along with being the only child of a rich and powerful man," I begin sadly. "But I always found a way to make it feel normal. I'm a pretty adaptable person, I think. I've moved around so many times, I got really good at making friends wherever I go. I'm friendly, but I do okay by myself, too. I get lonely sometimes, but I deal with it. The expensive private institutions my dad sent me to for education had very high standards, and I always met them. I thought I could handle anything, you know? That's partly why I wanted to become a diplomat. So I could help others learn to cooperate and get along. So I could, you know, fix things that were broken. Build a better future. I've been given so much privilege in my life but I'm self-aware enough to know that I should give back somehow."

"Forgive me my ignorance, but that is surprising to hear," Nikolai admits. "I did not come from wealth. I never lived a life of leisure. I always assumed that the children of rich men were just as deplorable as their parents. I mean no offense."

I smile weakly. "None taken. I know what people must think of me."

He puts an arm around me. "But you're different. I can see that. You have a mind of your own, and your heart is in the right place," he says sagely. I look up at him, my eyes shining.

"You have no idea how nice it is to hear that," I tell him. "All my life, my father has tried to keep me as sheltered and vapid and clueless as possible. I see that now. All the moving around, the lavish vacations, the shallow gifts. He wanted to make me soft and stupid."

"And compliant," Nikolai adds.

"Yes. Exactly," I verify, still amazed at how he seems to really get it.

"He wanted you to be so comfortable that you never question anything," he says.

"Yep. Which is why I'm sure he thought I would just accept this horrible betrothal without complaint. I'm such a fool. But I have to think that my father is just as ignorant of how terrible Uncle Liev is as I was. Surely he wouldn't try to knowingly marry me off to some disgusting pig of a man," I mutter, frowning.

"One would hope," Nikolai says grimly.

"Anyway, I'm sorry I got you dragged into this mess," I tell him. "I don't know what exactly you were planning to do hiding out in the hedges like that, but I apologize for jeopardizing your... your mission. Or whatever you call it."

"Think nothing of it. You needed my help. What kind of coward would I be to have let you fall with no one to catch you? If I ever become the kind of man to turn away a beautiful woman in need of help, I will never look be able to look at myself in the mirror again," says Nikolai. "Regardless of how or why we ended up in those hedges together, I will not abandon you now, Anastasia. I told you I would take care of you, and I meant it."

My heart surges with affection and appreciation as I look up at him. Nikolai is still a mystery to me. I don't know who he is, really, or where he came from. I don't know what his intentions were when we met, but I know deep in my soul that I can trust him. Completely. He will never hurt me. In fact, as I recall with a twinge of painful longing, he is the only man I have ever known who could show me such indescribable pleasure.

And suddenly, I know exactly what I need right now. I know what will help me get through this terrifying ordeal. I don't know what the morning's light will bring, but tonight, I want to wrap myself up in Nikolai's strong arms and let him take my body however he wants to.

His blue eyes seem to almost glow with understanding. He knows what I want without my ever having to even open my mouth and say it. Nikolai slowly reaches to cup my cheek in his huge hand, his thumb tracing gently over my full bottom lip. My body tingles with warmth, with need, and he leans in to kiss me gently. His lips press against mine and I sigh into the kiss, feeling every ounce of tension in my body melt away as he holds me. His hands slide down my neck, my arms, my chest, all the way down to grasp my hips. Nikolai softly urges me to stand up, and guides me over to straddle him, climbing up onto his lap with my legs bent around his waist. As he kisses me, his tongue pushes inside my mouth and I moan, giving in to the waves of intoxicating lust. I have never felt like this before. So ravenous. So desperate for touch.

His hands slide down to grope my ass through my jeans as he gently rolls his hips. I inhale sharply when I realize that I can feel his hard, hot cock pressing against my ass as we rock together, kissing and folding into each other's arms. I want him. All of him. And I am willing to give all of myself to Nikolai, too. Right now. Tonight.

But just as the heat is building ever higher between us, an annoying sound splits the air, jolting us both out of the moment. It's a high-pitched chiming noise, and through the haze of lust, it occurs to me that it's my ringtone. My stupid cell phone is ringing in my back pocket.

"Shit," I murmur, sliding off of Nikolai's lap and reaching around to grab the phone. He watches silently as I check the screen. My eyes go wide and I look up at him with horror. "Oh my god. It's my father calling!" I gasp.

"Answer it," Nikolai says.

"What? Are you crazy?" I ask, shocked.

"It will be worse if you don't answer. Just lie. Tell him you felt ill and needed to go home. Tell him you caught a cab. Anything," he suggests. I bite my lip, unsure if I can follow through with what he's asking. I never lie to my father. He's never given me a good reason to.

But I know Nikolai is right. With a groan, I slide the screen open and press the phone to my ear. "Hello?" I murmur quietly.

"Anastasia Nestorevna Koroleva!" my father bellows angrily into my ear.

"Hi, Daddy," I whisper.

"What the hell is your problem? Where are you? Mr. Ovechkin is furious! How dare you disobey me? Running away from your fiance, absconding with a strange man like some low-class whore! What were you thinking?" he shouts, his voice so loud it's nearly hoarse. I tremble, my blood running cold. My father has never spoken to me this way in my life.

"I-I'm sorry, Daddy," I mumble.

"Sorry? *Der'mo*. Damn right you will be sorry when I get my hands on you! How could you do this to Liev? How could you do this to me? Have you lost your mind?" he demands.

"I just-- I just can't do it. I can't marry Liev. I'm sorry. It's not right," I speak up weakly.

"What do you mean 'not right'? He is your fiance. Your betrothed. You have no choice in the matter, Anastasia. You are my daughter and you will marry whomever I choose!" he spits.

"Daddy, he's not the man you think he is!" I exclaim. "Uncle Liev-- Mr. Ovechkin-- he's a bad guy! He's an abuser. He treats his staff like cattle. He hunts endangered animals. He is friends with

Theodore Harrington, for god's sake! I saw proof that--"

"Now, you listen to me," Daddy interrupts, his voice a low growl. "I don't give a damn what you think you know about Liev Ovechkin or his friends or his hobbies. It's none of your business. It doesn't matter. He could be a serial killer for all I care, it still does not give you the right to disobey me."

My jaw drops. I look over at Nikolai, who is staring off into space with a look of barely-contained rage on his face. I know he can hear every word of this.

"You mean... you knew? All this time, you knew Uncle Liev was a jerk and a criminal and you still want me to marry him? I am your daughter. Your only child," I splutter in disbelief.

"Exactly. You are my daughter, and that gives me the right to give you away to whomever I please," Daddy says coldly. "I have given you everything you could ever ask for. I have set you up for an easy, luxurious life of leisure as the wife of a powerful man. And this is how you repay me: by throwing it back in my face. Now, for the last time, tell me where you are."

Tears sting in my eyes and roll down my cheeks. I'm so confused, torn between anger, pain, shock, and pure sorrow. "No," I tell him firmly, trying to keep my voice even. "I won't tell you where I am. In fact, I am going to hang up right now."

"Anastasia, don't you dare," he warns me, but I don't listen. I end the call, turn off my phone, and throw it across the room. It bounces harmlessly on the bed, and I crumple to the floor, feeling as though the entire universe is collapsing on top of me.

NIKOLAI

I see bodies break on a regular basis, but it's rare I watch a soul shatter in such a gut-wrenching way. By the time Ana collapses, I am already halfway across the room to her, extending an arm and putting a hand on her shoulder as I crouch down beside her, mixing my shushing with the sounds of her sobs.

"Don't tell me it's okay!" she snaps, swatting my hand, though it doesn't budge. "There's no way this is okay, Nikolai!"

"I wasn't going to say it was," I say in a slow, soothing tone. She looks up at me with red-rimmed eyes. She sniffles, but there's anger and rage written all over those beautiful features. "Because it isn't."

"Are you serious?"

"Do I look like I'm joking?" I say, giving her a steady, firm gaze.

She shakes her head and sniffs, wiping tears away. "I just don't get a lot of sympathetic ears from people like you."

"People like me?" I ask with a wry smile.

"You know what I mean," she says.

And I do.

She means men in the bratva, the kinds of men who have run so much of her life before. But there is a difference with me. The others in the bratva, so many of them are in this for the money, just to climb a different kind of ladder, stepping on the lives of ordinary people as they go. I am here for a different reason.

I'm here for vengeance.

Ana stands up and starts pacing the room, visibly shivering for a moment as she works through the horrifically alien emotions of having your whole view of the world changed in a matter of seconds.

"I'm just a pawn to him," she says. "He doesn't even care for me, does he? That piece of shit just seems me as a bride to be given away! I thought...I thought..."

She pauses by the foot of the bed, putting a hand on it to take a moment and gather herself before she starts pacing again.

"I trusted him," she says, holding back tears. "I trusted that he would always have my interests at heart. He always said he loved me. I can't fucking believe I trusted him!"

"A girl should be able to trust her own parent," I say, "but that is often not the case."

"The hell it isn't," she snaps. "I just can't...*why*? Why would he do something like this, especially when he knows what kind of man Unc- what kind of man Liev Ovechkin is."

"I have worked for these men for a long time, Ana," my voice rumbles. "They care only for money, nothing more."

She glares at me while she paces, but she needs to hear this.

"Human lives are nothing to these people" I say. "They're just another resource, like you. These are sociopaths unable to see others as being the same as them."

"And what about you?" she snaps.

"I chose this path in life for a reason," I say, deadly serious. "And believe me when I tell you I've suffered my own loss. A heinous loss that is the spur in my side every day that I pick and choose what work to take for these monsters." I have never come this close to explaining my life to anyone, and I don't know how it can come so easily to me around Ana, but the aura around her is irresistible. "Your father and Liev Ovechkin are my enemies, and now, they both know it. But you, Ana," I say, looking down at her and caressing her face, "you and I are not as unalike as you might think."

Her jaw tightens, but after a moment, she nods.

"Fine," she says. "If we're on the same side, then let's act like it. I'll tell you everything I can about Liev."

She starts to describe his daily schedule to me, all while pacing. She goes through much of the same information I already knew, but some details are new, and I make note of them as she speaks. There's such an intensity in her eyes as she rants, and I can taste the betrayal she feels in the air. She even starts to describe some of the times Liev and her father worked together.

Even mention of some business they took care of in Siberia, too close to my hometown to be a coincidence. My suspicions grow closer to being confirmed every passing day.

"My own daddy," she sobs, and she balls up a fist like she wants to punch a wall. I step up to her and catch her by the elbow. She spins around and tries to wrench free from me, gritting her teeth and jerking her arm, but I wrap my arms around her in a tight hug, pulling her into my chest. Immediately, she starts sobbing, melting into my embrace like there's nothing else in the world for her to cling to. Because for once in this spoiled girl's life, there really isn't.

"Let it out," I say in the gentlest tone I can. I am a killer, not a comforter, but I can at least try to be both. "Don't bottle up your anger."

"I don't want to be angry," she says after a few

moments she takes to collect herself. She looks up at me with eyes that are hurt yet defiant, and she shows no impulse to pull away from me.

"Then what *do* you want, Anastasia?" I ask, and I can feel her heart pounding faster and faster as I hold her.

Without a second thought, she jumps up and kisses me, and my hands go under her ass to hold her against me.

There's no thought, no more planning or deliberating, no more therapy, just action. I walk us back to the bed as she pushes her tongue against my lips, and I let her in. She only has time to explore me briefly before I bite at her lip, and I sit us down on the mattress, holding her firmly against my body as we lie down together.

My head is swimming with desire. The ferocity in this girl is like nothing I have ever seen before in a civilian. Her energy is infectious, and now more than ever before, I feel that I must make her mine. My body is still pulsing with need from the interrupted session we had in the car, and this time, nothing on heaven or earth could stop me from releasing that need.

She moans and whimpers like a prisoner as we touch each other. I have to restrain my strength as I work her shirt off, and her bra comes next. I push her flat on her back and straddler her, whipping my belt off as my eyes glare down at her exposed breasts. A low growl escapes me at the sight of them.

Everything about Ana is delicious, everything perfect. I've only known her for a few hours, truthfully, but we move against each other as if we've been together for years. She starts to reach up, but I grab both her wrists with my hands and force her down, pinning her to the bed. My cock is so swollen and tight against my pants that it aches.

My face goes to her left breast, and I take as much of it into my mouth as I can. My tongue rolls over the stiff nipple, and she lets out another cracking squeak as I toy with it. The tip of my tongue flicks it until it's so stiff that it feels hard, and I then take it between my teeth and toy with it gingerly. She squirms in my grasp as my sharp teeth play with the most sensitive of skin, but I never get too rough--I am in control, and she knows it. I play with both her breasts like this, and whenever one of them isn't in my mouth, my eyes are on it, watching it stiffen and move as she pushes her body up, trying desperately to feel as much of me as she can.

My mouth works its way up to her neck, and I start sucking on the smooth flesh there as I take her hands and guide them to my front. I hold her by the wrists and let her slowly feel my pecs and abs. She gropes them and savors the feeling. I'm like a cliff face with just enough give, just enough warmth and softness to make her feel safe and protected. She needs me. She craves everything I have to offer, including my protection. But I mean to give her so much more, as much as she can handle and then some.

Once I have guided her hands past my abs, I let them feel the buttons of my pants, and I release her wrists. She takes the cue and starts to unbutton them, but she stops halfway through, looking up at me with pleading eyes.

"I want to see it," she whispers. I nod and sit up on my knees, letting her see her work. The buttons come undone at last, and she pulls my pants down enough to let my cock spring out, fully erect and aiming right at her.

The sight makes her gasp, and the hungry look on her face fills me with desire for her.

"Touch it," I instruct her. "Feel what's going to be inside you."

She does, and she touches me as if my manhood is precious jewels. Her fingers are soft and warm, and I can feel just how much so they are as they caress my cock, working their way down to the balls. She explores me with such innocent wonder and yet such base desire.

"Do you want this?" I ask as she runs her hand up and down my cock, and I let it twitch up to attention to let her know the effect she can have on it. She looks up at me with doe-eyes and nods, mouth open.

I work my way down her, and she helps me pull

her pants off her, tossing them to the side and leaving her utterly naked.

"Do you know how delicious you look to me?" I growl in a husky tone, reaching down and running my hands from her sides to her hips to her round ass, squeezing her hungrily.

"Show me," she begs, and I don't want to hold back any longer.

I scoop her legs into my hands, and I drape them over my shoulders and let my shaft rest between her lips. I haven't even penetrated her yet, but her eyes roll back into her head as she feels me grind against her with the soft underside of my cock.

"This is nothing," I growl. "You have much to learn."

I bring the tip of my cock up to her wet lips. They're so soaking with desire that I can slide in with almost no effort, but I hold her there, making eye contact with her. Slowly, I push my cock into her. As soon as my crown is past her soft lips, she lets out a sharp moan, and I feel honey all around my shaft. Inch by inch, I enter her, until a third of my cock is inside her.

"Fuck, you're tight," I groan.

"I've never had anything like this in me," she gasps, and I see that even though not even half of me is in her, she's already gripping the sheets, bracing herself. I hold her hips, gentle and firm, and I guide my cock further in. Halfway in, I pull back out almost to the tip, and I start to rock back and forth. The sighs she lets out fill the room, and they make me stiffen harder and swell larger with each passing second. Back and forth, I let my bulging crown grind against her insides, exploring her deep pussy, and soon, I start to delve deeper.

"There's more?" she gasps when she looks up and realizes how little of my cock is inside her. "Will it all fit?"

"We'll see, won't we?" I growl, and I feel her pussy tighten around me. I start to get more aggressive, going a little deeper with each thrust. "Stay relaxed," I tell her. "I won't hurt you."

"What if I want you to?" she whispers.

My cock twitches, and I feel a bead of precum well up at the tip at those words. I groan, and my grip on her hips tightens.

"You're playing with fire now, girl," I rumble.

I rock into her harder, and soon, two thirds of my cock are inside her. Before long, I hear my heavy, sore balls slap against her ass, and she yelps as I hit that most sensitive spot inside her.

"Oh god!" she gasps, and I feel her tightening, preparing for an orgasm. I'm not even trying, and this girl is about to lose herself around me. But I won't let this moment go to waste. I start thrusting harder, getting more steady and hitting that same spot over and over again, and within seconds, she lets out a sharp cry as she comes.

At the shuddering feeling of the release of tension in her pussy, I start to buck into her freely. My cock is thick and ribbed with veins, and I want her to experience it at full capacity. As I guide her through the orgasm, I start thrust into her harder and faster, balls hitting her ass and flesh grinding against soaking flesh as her mouth falls open. I'm rendering this girl a hot mess, and I've never wanted anything more in a single moment.

I fuck her in this position until her orgasm subsides, and then I pull out of her. She gasps, looking up at me in surprise.

"Did you finish?" she asks. I chuckle.

"No, girl," I growl. "Get on your knees."

She clumsily turns over and obeys, presenting her ass for me in such an enticing way that I could come on her right then. I'm done being sensual and slow, though. I want to claim her, and I'm going to take her for *my* pleasure. I hold her hips tight and ram my cock up into her.

She lets out a sharp cry of delight, her head falling and hair scattering over her like a curtain as I start to buck into her wantonly. We have no protection, nothing between our sexes as I rut into her with animal vigor.

Ever since I saw her in the airport, I have wanted this. I have trained my body to obey my commands, but this is the one that I will take from it. Body, soul, and mind have nothing but desire for this girl, and she needs me desperately. My whole cock slides up into her with ease, and I feel her tight around me from crown to thick base. We seem to fit each other perfectly. Each time I slide up into her she whimpers, and I can feel her getting tighter by the second.

I'm not taking my time anymore. I thrust up into her fiercely, and I feel her pulse with need as my precum spills into her. I feel my virile balls swinging under us, and at last, I decide it's time to bring both of us to the end.

I rut into her with deadly precision, releasing all restraints on my body and its functions. Soon, I spill over the edge, and I start to lose my rhythm. She knows what's coming too, and as soon as she realizes that, it's all over for her.

I look down at that gorgeous sight of my rock-hard, muscular body fucking into her soft form, her ass shaking with every thrust, and I lose all control. My cock stiffens, my balls tighten, and I feel the first shot of seed jet into her at the same time that she lets out another cry of orgasm.

I groan along with her, holding her close to me and keeping her pinned to my hips as I spend my seed inside her. Shot after shot of my hot, pearly fluid spills into her, more than I've released in a long time. Our juices mix together beautifully, and neither of us hold anything back. The sound of our lovemaking fills the room until both of us finish. I remain in her, hard as a rock for several more seconds, massaging my come into her while she gasps for breath and whimpers in soft delight.

Finally, I pull out, and we both collapse onto the bed.

We're both left panting and exhausted afterward, and I have never felt more fulfilled in as long as I can remember. She is everything I imagined and so, so much more. I turn my head to look at her, and I feel as if an arrow has shot me through the heart at the sight of her sleepy, satisfied face smiling at me, half-buried in sheets.

"That was...more than I ever imagined," she says, and the sound of her thick voice makes my cock twitch as though already braced for more.

I start to reply, but a sudden buzzing catches her attention. She sits up like a lightning bolt and picks up her phone, glancing between it and me.

"Daddy," she whispers, anger coming back to her face. I feel angry, too. That monster of a man is intruding on our golden moment, spoiling the joy we feel suspended between us. She hesitates for a few moments, then slowly answers the phone and puts it to her ear.

"What?" she snaps. There's a pause, and I can't keep a smile off my face. I can perfectly visualize Nestor Koroleva's face souring at the sound of his daughter mouthing off to her.

"You want to be treated like an adult? Fine," I hear his bitter voice through the receiver. Even with all her anger, I can see Ana's hurt at the tone. "If you won't tell me where you are, then let's meet in the middle. I want to arrange a meeting."

I feel like I'm going to be sick.

I'm sitting in an upscale French bistro, possibly the only truly fancy restaurant in this tiny, podunk country town. It's certainly the only one fancy enough to require a parking garage, since it's located in a shopping plaza with some ritzy little boutiques and artisan candle shops. Typical American small town stuff, not that I have ever spent much time in a small town in my lifetime. Especially not in America. Sure, I've gone on some short day trips to cute little villages and hamlets in various European countrysides, but never on Long Island. But my father wanted to meet up and talk in person. In fact, he demanded it. And I have never been good at telling my father no. Of course, that's mostly because he has always treated me well enough that I never needed to. Until now.

Still, I did not want to give him the upper hand here. I need to be in a bargaining position, and if there's one thing I have learned from my father over the years, it's how to establish dominance. All this time, when my dad thought I was just some airheaded, spoiled little girl who was too busy shopping for a new Louis Vuitton handbag to pay attention to anything else, I have actually been watching him much more closely than anyone would have guessed by looking at me. I know how I appear to most people. I look every bit the part of a pampered little princess who has never had to think for herself or make big decisions. I look demure and sweet and innocent, and I suppose to an extent, I am all of those things. But that's not all I am.

I'm also resourceful. And smart. And attentive. So while I sat next to my father in first class as we rode a train through the picturesque Spanish landscape or what have you, I listened to his conversations with investors and competitors. His legal team. His subordinates. Maybe at first, when I was a little younger, I didn't listen on purpose. In fact, when I was a little girl I used to tune out his business calls on purpose. Listening to him rant and rave about stocks and risk versus reward tactics was pretty dull to me as a child. But once I got a little older, I started to quietly pay attention. I made notes, sometimes just in my head, and sometimes actually on paper or on a memo in my cell phone. I noticed his strategies, internalized them. Stowed them away for safekeeping, even though I never imagined there would come a day when I might actually make use of the stuff I picked up from him. Now, though, I am starting to see the benefits of growing up in close proximity to one of the world's most formidable businessmen. I know the ins and outs of business negotiations. I know my father's instincts, because some of them are my instincts, as well. I know what he's doing. I learned it from watching him all these years.

I plan to beat him at his own game.

Step one? Never let your opponent get you on his home turf. Home team advantage is applicable to more than just football. So when my father called me wanting to meet up and talk, it only made sense for me to insist that he come all the way out here to quaint little Roslyn, on Long Island, rather than agree to meet him at our home in Sands Point or at the hotel room on the Upper East Side. He fought me on that, of course, but I stood my ground. Finally, I broke him down and he reluctantly accepted my plan to meet up at this cheesy French bistro complete with a second-rate jazz band and waiters in black. I may not be from Roslyn, but I know it better just from my brief time here than my father does, that's for sure. He doesn't mess around with small towns. They don't have much to offer him. In this case, that gives me the advantage.

Step two? Don't lay all your cards out on the

table before your opponent does. That means that I will refuse to tell him anything about Nikolai or the crazy escape he facilitated for me last night until Daddy agrees to tell me everything about Liev and their little exchange. I want to know why exactly he wants to marry me off to a man like Liev. And I refuse to believe that it's all about giving me a bright future. I don't need a fat, snobbish, manipulative husband to give me that. If I were allowed to go off to college or an internship or whatever on my own, I could make my way all by myself. This isn't the Victorian era. I don't need to marry for money, and I sure as hell don't need my father to arrange a marriage for me against my will. There has got to be something bigger than a simple marriage at stake here. Why Liev Ovechkin? Why not one of the myriad other rich guys my father is friends with? What does Uncle Liev have over my father? Is it pure greed? Blackmail? A business trade: a daughter for a yacht or something? I shudder to think that something so superficial could be the reason why, but at this point, I'm feeling pretty disillusioned in this father-daughter dynamic. I don't have much faith left in him.

Step three? Outdress and impress. This one's simple. I know what my dad dresses like. I could probably describe to you most of his wardrobe from memory. Now, my harrowing escape from the Ovechkin manor left me barefoot, with ripped and torn clothes. That's no way to dress for a negotiation. So this morning, Nikolai retrieved the car from the mechanic, fully repaired, and we went to one of the many clothing boutiques in the area. I flashed my daddy's credit card, but rather unsurprisingly, he had already called the credit card company to put a hold on the account. So Nikolai graciously bought me a summery new dress, a cardigan, and a pair of strappy sandals. I got my hair, makeup, and nails done at the salon next to the boutique. Now, sitting at the corner table in this French bistro, I might not look like a million bucks, but I at least look like a good several thousand. Youth always beats wisdom, my dad told me once, and in this case, my youthful good looks will automatically tip the scales in my favor, even though he's going to be wearing Armani and I'm wearing some nobody's brand. I have the confidence and the bravado to pull this off.

At least, that's what I'm telling myself as I sit here nervously waiting for Daddy to show up. The waiter has already offered me wine three times, but I'm underage, so as much as I would love a sip of wine to take the edge off, I've said no. Daddy has thought ahead. I can see what he's doing. I have the upper hand by staking out the restaurant first, but he's countering with a well-known tactic: to keep me waiting. The more restless and impatient I get, the less powerful I feel. Daddy has shown up hours late to meetings before, just to keep his opponent on his toes. But me? I'm prepared for that. I have spent lots of time waiting around on him to come collect me, to turn up for our scheduled luncheons. It doesn't bother me.

When he walks in at half past four, dressed to the nines with a wry smile on his face, I'm ready for him. I stand and greet him with a kiss to the cheek, as if everything is totally normal. I want to keep him guessing. However, there is still that little daddy's girl inside of me who just wants to hug him, to cry in his arms and beg him to tell me everything will be okay.

But I know better now. I can't trust him. I want to, but I can't.

"Hi, Daddy," I greet him as we sit down across from each other. I've done another subtle trick; I'm sitting with my back to the wall so I can see the entire restaurant, while he's facing me, which means that anyone could sneak up behind him at any time and he wouldn't know. It's just a little thing to set him off-balance and make him just that tiny bit more nervous.

He didn't know he was teaching me all these years, but I have learned well.

"*Privet, myshka*," he says, folding his hands together on the white tablecloth. He raises an eyebrow as he looks around the restaurant, wrinkling his nose slightly. "You could not have picked a slightly less, ahh, blue-collar establishment for this meeting?"

"What's wrong, Daddy? Do all these honest people make you uncomfortable?" I ask, tilting my head to one side and giving him a placid smile. "I tried to book us a table in a den of snakes, but they weren't taking any reservations. I apologize. I know you would feel more at home there."

He narrows his eyes at me, clearly taken aback by my acidic tone.

"So, Anastasia, what is your intention this afternoon? What is it that you want?" he asks.

"I want the truth. About Liev. About this engagement. About you," I tell him.

He chuckles good-naturedly as the waiter comes over to take our order. Daddy orders a dry martini and escargot. The waiter looks petrified.

"Sir, we don't serve escargot here," he admits.

Daddy leans back in his chair, glaring at him. "This is a French restaurant, *da*?"

"Y-Yes, sir, but--"

"You might want to rethink your brand, then," says my father icily. "Bring me something edible, if you think your chef can manage that. Surprise me."

The waiter nods nervously and looks at me. I give him an apologetic smile. "I'll just have a soda and the brie plate, please," I tell him. He looks relieved and putters off. I turn my attention back to my father.

"My dear daughter, I believe the two of us can come to an armistice," he says graciously. "After all, we want the same thing, do we not?"

"And what is that?" I prompt.

"Your happiness, of course," he replies. I snort.

"Yeah, right."

"You have a misguided idea of what it takes to be happy, but I will take the blame for that. Perhaps I have spoiled you *too* much. I made life too easy for you, and now your ego is bigger than your intellect. What a shame," Daddy muses, clucking his tongue.

"Well, if you're so worried about my intellect, why would you marry me off to some crusty old man rather than let me further my education?" I counter.

"Because, my little mouse, I am a shrewd businessman, and I know how to recognize a good offer when I see it," he remarks cryptically.

"A good offer?" I repeat, frowning as the waiter silently sets down my soda and Daddy's martini before scurrying away. "So you admit that this is about money? Is that it? You sold me off to Liev like I'm just another one of your assets?"

"My, my, you certainly have a most unromantic mind, don't you?" he scolds, taking a sip of his drink. He winces at the taste. "And you could not have chosen a restaurant with a more palatable selection of liquor?" he complains.

I lean forward, trying to intimidate him. "If you

think that drink tastes bitter, you'd better man up, because I have a much more difficult pill for you to swallow, Daddy," I whisper.

He looks amused. "And what is that, dear daughter?"

I take a deep breath and launch into the speech I've been reciting in my head all day. "I refuse to marry Liev. I won't do it. You can't make me. I'm legally an adult, and I don't have to do what you ask of me anymore. You can cut off my credit card, you can be angry with me, you can do whatever you want, but I'm putting my foot down. I don't want to marry that criminal."

Daddy rolls his eyes. "Criminal? Let's not play the moral superiority card."

"Why not? Why is Mr. Ovechkin allowed to do the horrible things he does without consequences? What makes him so special?" I demand in a low voice.

"Money," he answers simply. "And power. Come now, I thought you were at least smart enough to realize that."

"But it's not fair," I reply. "You shouldn't give him a free pass just because of his money or his status. That's wrong, Daddy, and you know it."

He shrugs. "There is no right or wrong in business, *myshka*. There are only losers and winners. Do you want to be a loser?"

I shake my head, totally in shock. "You're not the man I thought you were," I mutter.

Daddy chuckles. "Then you are an even bigger fool than I knew."

That's it. I've had enough. I stand up suddenly and throw down my napkin. Daddy regards me placidly as I glare at him. "Daddy, with all due respect, screw you. I-I'm not going to marry Liev. I'm going to walk out of here now, and you can't stop me."

He leans back and shrugs. "I suppose you're right. Go, have your little meltdown. But don't come crying back to Papa when you realize you've lost," he sneers.

Before even waiting to cancel my order, I storm out of the restaurant in tears, my hands curled into fists at my sides. I can't believe how cold and cruel he is, how totally unlike the father I've loved he seems to be. That's not the man I have looked up to my whole life. The curtain has been yanked back, and now the ugly truth is on full display. I'm hurt. I'm confused. I'm shocked. And I'm angry at myself for not seeing it sooner. I should have known.

I make my way up to the parking garage and step out of the elevator with tears streaming down my face. I can't remember where exactly we parked, but my mind is too mixed up to figure it out. I start wandering aimlessly through the labyrinth of vehicles and cold concrete, my heart racing like mad. As

I turn a corner, a flash of bright, searing pain rips through my body.

I don't even have time to figure out what happened before I crumple to the ground, my head spinning. There's a dull, horrible ache at the back of my head, and I feel sick to my stomach. I hear heavy footsteps and a grunt, and I turn to look up just as a tall, scowling man with a familiar face lifts a plank of wood over his head to bring down upon me. I gasp and try to wiggle away, jerking out of dodge just as the plank smacks the concrete floor. I'm under attack! The man glares at me in annoyance, and in the back of my mind, through the pulsing agony, I remember who he is. I can't conjure up a name, but I know he's one of my father's associates. A junior business partner of some kind.

I have known him since I was a child, and he's trying to hurt me.

He raises the wood plank up again and I instinctively dive down, curling up into a ball and shielding my head with my arms, bracing for the inevitable assault. But then there's an earth-shattering crack, and I let out a scream. Something warm and wet sprays over my body, and I open one eye to see that the man is no longer standing over me. Someone else is there.

Nikolai!

He offers me his hand, a dark look on his face. "Come on! We have to go!" he orders.

Still dazed, I slowly take his hand. He yanks me up to my feet and I notice two things in quick, horrifying succession. First of all, the man who attacked me is lying facedown on the ground, a dark pool gathering at the back of his skull, matting in his hair. Secondly, there's a splash of bright, vibrant red down my front. Blood. It's blood.

I put two and two together and open my mouth to scream, but Nikolai puts his hand over my mouth and shakes his head fervently. Without another word, he lifts me over his shoulder and begins to dash across the parking garage. Hanging over his shoulder, I'm dizzy and nauseated, watching as the pool of blood grows wider and wider surrounding the body we left behind. I'm too horrified to say a word, my body going into shock. Nikolai shoves me into the passenger seat of his black car, tosses a towel over me for the blood, and throws the engine into gear. As we peel out of the parking garage and out onto the back roads of this sweet, quaint small town, I stare over at Nikolai with wide eyes and a slack jaw.

Who the hell is he? Can I trust him? I thought I could, but...

I just watched him kill a man without a second's hesitation.

Who *is* this guy?

She is in shock as I load her into the passenger's seat of my car. Her eyes are wide and staring, and her hands are starting to shake ever so slightly. Her form is so small and seems so fragile, now more than ever. She is a living paradox. There is much courage and strength in her, but even so, she is so very human, and she still has the conscience and sensitivity for this kind of ugly business that I abandoned long ago.

Dealing with her is both strange and humbling.

She sits there numbly as I guide her legs in, and I bring the seatbelt down across her body to click into place before shutting the door and hurrying around to the driver's side. A moment later, I peel out of the parking lot, and we take off down the road.

New York traffic is dense, but that works to my advantage today. I can disappear into the sea of metal and rumbling engines, slinking through the city like just another dot out of millions. There is a reason that many mafias have thrived in this city for so many years.

Many minutes pass in utter silence as I drive. She just stares forward, in shock. It is frustrating to watch at first, but I soon rein myself in and put myself in her position. Up until a few days ago, the most stressful thing in this girl's life was having to leave some new friends behind on her way to yet another staggeringly rich manor in yet another European country. The most excitement she knew was the thrill of getting flirted with by another young man her age on a marble terrace at some luxurious party. She comes from an entirely different world than the one I am used to.

"Tell me what you saw," I say after enough time has passed between us in silence. She blinks a few times, as if surprised by the question, and she turns to look at me blankly.

"What?"

"Tell me what you saw," I repeat, more slowly.

"You know what I saw," she says. There's a rueful edge to her tone, and I nod.

"Yes, I do," I admit. "But I asked you to tell me anyway. I want you to say it. I want you to hear it in your own voice."

She stares at me a long time. There are a lot of emotions in those gorgeous eyes. She wants to figure out what I'm getting at, but at the same time, she wonders if this is some sick game to me. But I am firm, and I say no more to distract her. She finally parts her soft lips and struggles to find the words.

"A body," she says.

I make a gesture for her to say more. She swallows and clenches her eyes shut.

"Nikolai…"

"I know it is hard," I say softly. "But this will help. What did you see?"

"I saw the body of the man you killed," she finally forces herself to say. "I saw him in a pool of his own blood. You killed the man who was trying to kill me, and I saw him dead."

I nod, satisfied. "He was trying to kidnap you, actually. You're worth more alive than dead. But nonetheless, well done. You're stronger than I was."

That takes her by surprise. She stares at me again, then gives her head a little shake.

"Wait, what? What are you talking about?"

I take a deep breath, then let it out even more slowly as our car moves through traffic somewhat more swiftly. The smell of these leather seats and the comfort of the vehicle are nice, but they are not all I have ever known. I have never shared my past with anyone else, but I feel that the time has come. If I cannot use my past experiences to help someone who is hurting, then what kind of monster am I?

"I said you are stronger than I was when someone posed the same question to me," I say.

"When did you have to answer a question like that?"

"When I was a child," I say. "I might have been nine or ten. So long ago that the memories are somewhat of a blur."

"In Russia?" she asks hesitantly, and I nod slowly.

"I come from near a city in Siberia called Omsk. I grew up on the outskirts, in a poor area. More like a village near Omsk than anything else. I thought I had an ordinary childhood. We had little money, nothing like the kind of wealth here in America, but I never went hungry either. I had a younger brother. He was smaller than me, and much more frail."

She watches me with attentive, enraptured eyes, but even she can tell where this is going.

"He got sick," I say. There is little emotion in my voice, not because I do not have it, but because of the gravity the memory holds for me. I have had to mute myself over the years. "My parents could not afford treatment, I knew. Even back then, I knew how poor we were. Children notice things more than parents give them credit for. But still, somehow, we took him to a hospital in Omsk to get treatment. I remember being told he had a rare condition that was expensive to treat. I remember my mother crying. He didn't pull through, in the end."

"Nikolai..." she trails off, staring at me.

"Things got worse after that," I say, turning off onto the highway. "My mother started working as well. Papa took a second job. I never saw him. Men in suits came to visit, often. Papa always looked worried when they came. They spoke to him in soft voices, but there was malice in them. One day, they went out to the car to get groceries while I stayed inside. I heard an explosion."

She puts her hands to her mouth, but my face is placid as I watch the road. This has played over a million times in my head, and it always will, exactly the same way. It is as vivid as if it happened yesterday.

"It was a car bomb," I say. "I ran out and saw the wreckage. I called the police. They didn't come alone. One of the men in suits was with them. He asked me that question while I was crying into his arms. 'Tell me what you saw.' I couldn't answer him. I was not strong enough. He told me he was my uncle. That his father had plans for me. That I was coming to America, where I would have work waiting for me."

"That's how you were recruited," she breathes. I give a single nod. She has all but forgotten the trauma of what she saw, so I accomplished what I wanted to do, but I also feel strangely relieved to tell it to someone else. "But why did you stay with them?"

"There is no leaving the bratva, under most

conditions," I say. Silence falls between us again for a long time as we drive.

Finally, we reach the suburb I've been making my way toward. It's a tacky area, one of those neighborhoods where all the houses are nearly identical boxes, with sod lawns and white walls.

"Where are we?" she finally asks, peering around at the houses.

"The safe place I meant to take you before," I say, and I pull into the driveway of one of the houses as the garage door opens before me. I pull in slowly and close the door behind us before getting out and breathing in the artificial air. "We call places like this a safehouse."

"Why?"

"Nobody knows about them," I say. "The bratva keeps tabs on where its members usually live, but those of us with enough money like to keep places like this to ourselves. Hard to trace, somewhere unassuming, where you're unlikely to run into a business partner. Come on, let's get settled."

"How long are we going to be here?" she asks as I open the door and let us inside. The house smells new, and all the walls are pristine, stark white. I grimace. This isn't my style at all, but it will do for now.

"Until I get some business sorted out," I say. "Why don't you go take a shower? I have some phone calls to make."

She gives me a reluctant look. Despite all that we've talked about, I can tell that the thoughts of what she has seen today are still very fresh in her mind, and she doesn't want to be alone. Hell, she must be surprised at herself for even coming with me. But I put a hand on her shoulder and give it a squeeze, nodding to her assuringly. She still hesitates, but she turns and heads deeper into the house to find the bathroom without another word.

After she leaves, I run my hand over my face and let out a deep breath. I am not prepared to handle a girl like Anastasia. This is going to be a long work in progress.

As soon as I hear the shower water running and don't think she's trying to eavesdrop on my conversation, I take out my phone and dial a number. I make my way to the window and peer outside briefly before turning around and making sure all the blinds are shut while I listen to the rings.

"Hello?" a gruff voice finally comes.

"It's me," I say.

"You're still alive," the voice says, mildly impressed. "You really stirred up the hive, you know."

"Can't imagine how," I say. "Can't a man go dark for a few days?"

"Not when Nestor's daughter goes missing too," the voice says. "But don't worry, the only ones who suspect it was you are the ones in our circle. But it's only a matter of time, comrade."

"I know," I say. "Stay focused. How are the party favors coming along?"

"Ready to go," he says.

"And the airline tickets?" I ask.

"Also prepared," he says. "You said we needed to hurry things along, so we have. Things are ready to go, but Liev isn't going to just come out into the open without a damn good reason after that little garden party of yours."

"I hope I don't have to explain why it was necessary," I say, and the voice chuckles.

"No need to worry, comrade, we're still behind you every step of the way. But we'll need the word soon. Very soon."

"And you'll have it," I say. "There's just one more piece of the puzzle I need to cover," I say, glancing in the direction of the shower.

"I understand, sir," he says. "Are you safe?"

"Yes," I say. "Both of us."

"Both? So it's true."

"It is," I say curtly. "You've all done well. I'll bring my end of the plan through for you. Just be patient for a little longer."

"You have my word," he says, and I end the call. There has been a lot of planning put into this, and I'm not going to let anything get in the way. But I'd rather do things the easy way rather than the hard way.

I realize the shower water has stopped, and I make my way to the master bedroom to peer in.

Ana is there, her hair soaking wet and her body wrapped in a towel, but she's leaning on the dresser and just staring into the mirror, her face blank and pale. I approach her quickly, and she flinches at my touch. I clench my jaw, and she looks up at me with wide eyes.

"I…"

"It's okay," I say softly, and tears run down her eyes as I hug her to me, feeling her wet hair soak my arms as her tiny frame shivers and sobs in my grasp. "You've been through some of the roughest days of your life, Anastasia. You are allowed to have a moment of weakness. Or five."

"I don't want to be weak," she says, bitterness in her voice. "I've been weak all my life, Nikolai! I'm always getting carted around the world, but I thought that was all I would ever be involved in. I can't…I don't want to have to break down every time something like this happens."

"You are better off without seeing bodies as often as I do, if that's what you're worried about," I say. "Don't fault yourself for that."

"It's just…" she starts, hesitating, "I think about the business my father is in, and the business that cost you your parents. You were so young…"

I can tell what she's thinking, and she isn't wrong. I don't want to tell her that her father had a hand in my parents' murder.

Even though I know it to be true.

It has been the single biggest motivator in my life: revenge. I want justice for the monsters who killed my parents.

Before they were rivals, Nestor and Liev worked together in their own prickly ways, and I know that both of them were involved in the death of my parents for a loan they could not pay back. A loan that could not even save my brother's life.

But how can I tell a girl like Ana that her own father is a true monster? She has heard nothing but his lies all her life, and she is only just now starting to learn a hint of the truth of the situation. She knows that her father cares little enough for her that he'd just trade her away as a resource. She heard that with her own ears.

But still, if I had heard that my father were a monster, I would have fought it. I would have dug my heels in and looked for any way to explain it away rather than accept that my whole world is a lie. There is no easy way to accomplish that. Hell, I may well be making an enemy out of my lover by telling her what really needs to happen. And if that is the price I must pay, then so be it.

Anastasia is starting to mean more to me than anything has in my life, but at the same time, I cannot let my plans fall to pieces just to protect Nestor. That would be unacceptable. There are more lives than my own on the line. Many more. Surely she will be able to see that.

I lose track of how long I hold Ana there, letting her get it all out before she wordlessly dries her hair off and starts to get dressed. After she has finished, she sits on the bed, rubbing her eyes and taking a deep breath as I step back into the room, peering down at her.

"Anastasia," I say in my deep, husky tone. "We need to talk."

She peers up at me steadily, but her jaw is set.

"You are more than just the daughter of Nestor Koroleva," I say. "Much more. You are a woman who is clever and decisive. You have potential. Much more than you know. I will not be like your father, keeping you in the dark. I want you to know exactly where we stand and what's going on here."

Her gaze is so steady and even that I feel like she can peer into my soul. Slowly, she nods, and I take a deep breath before ripping the bandaid off.

"Ana...your father needs to die."

ANASTASIA

The world around me starts to crumble away, all sights and sounds disintegrating into nothingness as I stand stock-still in the empty living room. The vaulted ceiling and cheap tile floors of the room fade away around me. The damp towel in my arms drops to the floor, and I start to feel lightheaded. Goosebumps pop up on my arms and legs as I stand there in my flimsy dress. The same dress I wore earlier today when I confronted my father at that stupid French bistro. I sat across from him, the man I have respected and idolized ever since I was a little girl, and defied him. I stood up for myself for the first time ever, the first time I've ever needed to. That was difficult enough, just facing up to the one authority figure who has dominated and reigned over every day of my eighteen years of life. I realize now how foolish I was to have ever trusted him. Why was I so willing to accept that his word was truth? All these years, I have trusted him with my whole heart, no matter how many times he abandoned me in favor of some flashy business trip or phone call with an associate. All the years of playing second fiddle to his career-- his criminal career, if I am to believe what Nikolai is suggesting to me right now.

But he's my father. He wouldn't hurt me. And he wouldn't hurt all those other people, either. Would he? It's hard enough to accept that Uncle Liev is a bad man, but my own father? My daddy who has doted on me and spoiled me since day one of my life?

Besides, he's all I have in the world. He has never let me live in one place long enough to build real, lasting relationships with friends my own age or anything. Hell, even the attendants and assistants he has hired to help and accompany me never lasted longer than six months to a year. Daddy has systematically taken away every single person I could have bonded with… except himself. He made himself the only one I could count on as a constant in my life, and even then he made himself scarce a lot of the time. Unreachable. Too wrapped up in the intricacies of the business world to make time for his only daughter.

It hits me like a meat cleaver to the face: I am already turning against him.

But I don't want to. I don't want to give up on the only family I have. He's always been my everything, the one person I can count on. The voice in the back of my head reminds me that I can't always count on him, though. How many times has he left me hanging?

"I'm so confused," I manage to croak out, staring blankly at the stark white wall.

I feel my legs starting to fold underneath me, giving up on me. My whole body, my entire mind, my heart and my soul-- they're all collapsing in on themselves under the weight of what Nikolai just said to me. Death is so permanent an answer to the questions I'm still too afraid, perhaps even too brainwashed, to ask. I somehow force myself to drag my gaze away from the wall to land on Nikolai's face. Those sharp cheekbones, the heavy brows and intense blue eyes. He is wearing an expression of grim resignation, but there's a flicker of pity in that stare.

He feels bad for me.

I feel the tiny shreds of what's left of my dignity swelling, puffing up indignantly. I am Anastasia Nestorevna Koroleva. I am the daughter of a very rich and powerful man. There is esteem and pride in my family name. Nobody should be able to look down on me, to regard me with pity. If there's one thing my father did give me, it's a healthy sense of pride. I don't want sympathy. I want the truth.

"Ana, listen to me," says Nikolai, but his voice sounds like it's far away. There's a loud rushing noise in my ears. I think it might be my own heartbeat, growing faster and louder as my mind drifts away to a safer place. I go rigid, standing there unable to move or think clearly. Distantly, I can feel my wet hair dripping down the back of my dress, giving me literal shivers down my spine. My thoughts scatter unhelpfully and a wave of vibrant memories come parading through the forefront of my brain.

Daddy, sitting on a brown leather couch in the living room of our house in Sands Point with a glass of vodka in one hand, smiling wryly as I sit on the floor, opening Christmas presents. I'm eight years old. He's got a cigar in his other hand, and he's watching me closely, gauging my reaction to the lavish gifts under the tree. I can still smell the pungent, nostalgic scent of the evergreen pine in my nose, accompanied by the sweeter smells of hot cocoa, peppermint candy canes, and a roast turkey in the oven. Faintly, there's the sound of our home chef humming "God Rest Ye Merry Gentlemen" as she putters around in the kitchen. He promises me that we can go sledding later, but instead he has the nanny take me sledding while he jets off to some warm, tropical "business" meeting near the Equator.

Daddy, dropping me off in London for boarding school when I was ten, assuring me that I would be fine without him. He's telling me how many friends I'm going to make, how happy and independent I will feel on my own. "Don't you want to be treated like an adult? This is your opportunity to be independent, to take care of yourself. But don't worry, I will come to visit you as often as I can manage," he promises me. It's a lie. He only comes to visit a few times a year, and he spends most of that time on the phone or passing me off to one of his assistants while he works. The first month at boarding school, I cry myself to sleep every night, I'm so lonely and scared. The academy's student counselor urges me to send him letters to assuage my loneliness and feelings of abandonment. He never writes me back. Not even once.

Daddy, lounging on the top deck of a yacht, surrounded by hot young women in bikinis, sipping a cocktail and flirting openly. Meanwhile, I'm on the lower deck, twelve years old, awkward and nervous and out of place in this crowd of tipsy adults drinking and doing drugs. I'm wearing a one-piece bathing suit and a floppy hat, and Daddy forgot to tell me to wear sunscreen. My skin is burning, turning bright pink. I watch in mingled horror and fascination as one of the grown-ups on the lower deck does a line of coke off the balcony banister. I wanted to come along so I wouldn't be left out, but I'm in way over my head. This is scary for me, but Daddy is too busy hitting on models half his age to look after me.

"Ana. Anastasia. Come on, speak to me. Say something. Anything," comes Nikolai's voice, slicing through the fog. His huge hands are on my shoulders, and he's gently shaking me, trying to bring me back to reality. I blink several times, tears trickling down my cheeks. I stare at him, those blue eyes brighter and deeper than the ocean.

I realize that I have somehow moved to sit down on the edge of the cheap couch, with Nikolai crouching in front of me, looking concerned. Nikolai is worried about me in a way my father never was. We have only just met, but he already cares about me more than Daddy does. He wants what's best for me. Even if that means…

"You can't," I murmur weakly. "You just can't do that."

His face falls, but he doesn't give up. "Ana, your father is a dangerous man. An evil man. He has committed crimes that would make Liev Ovechkin blush," he tells me gently.

Suddenly, fury overpowers my sadness. I shove him away bitterly. "No! You can't kill my father. He's all I have, Nikolai. He--he raised me. He's not the man you say he is," I protest.

His eyes flash with a warning. "You really think I would come to this conclusion if I didn't have a damn good reason?"

"I don't know!" I shout back, shrugging. "I don't know what you would do. I mean, I just watched you kill a guy for attacking me. Maybe you're just a violent man."

"Would you rather me have allowed that man to kidnap you?" he growls.

I glare at him. "Of course not. I don't know. None of this makes sense to me."

"I know. That's what I'm trying to explain. If you understood what kind of a man your father is, you would know why it has to be this way," Nikolai counters.

"What do you mean? What has he done that's bad enough to warrant killing him?" I cry out. "Isn't this America? Isn't it supposed to be innocent until proven guilty?"

He sighs. "You and I both know that powerful men like your father and Ovechkin aren't held to the same rules as the rest of society. They live outside of the rules. The courts can't stop them from continuing to hurt people. But a bullet to the heart can."

I gasp, feeling sick to my stomach again. "Oh my god, do you hear yourself? Do you even comprehend what you're suggesting to me right now? What is this: vigilante justice?"

He nods slowly. "Yes. That is precisely what it is. Justice."

"And that makes you, what? His judge, jury, and executioner?" I accuse angrily. "That's not how it works! He's my father, Nikolai, and I-I won't let you kill him."

"Ana, I'm doing this *for* you. To save you," he explains.

"From what? Sure, my dad might not be winning any Father of the Year awards anytime soon but does that really mean he has to die? No! It's absurd!" I reply.

"Nestor Koroleva is much more than just an unsatisfactory father," he says grimly. "It goes much, much deeper than that."

"Oh, really? How so? Tell me, Nikolai. What has my father done to deserve what you're suggesting he gets? Hmm? Let's think about it," I retort. "He's a businessman. A really, really successful one. So he's probably committed fraud or racketeering or some other bullshit white-collar crime, right? Who has he cheated out of their money?"

I can see that muscle in Nikolai's jaw clenching and unclenching as he struggles to maintain his composure. He's getting angry at me, I know it, but I can't let it go. Not when my father's life is at stake.

"It's far worse than that," he says quietly.

"How? Why? What could he have done? Look, I get it. He's not perfect. Hell, he's not even decent half the time, but he's no worse than any other millionaire in the world, right? Why don't you go after some other corporate bigwig?" I snap.

Nikolai stands up suddenly and takes a few furious strides across the room, pacing and refusing to make eye contact with me. I watch him, helpless and confused. My heart is being torn in two directions. On the one hand, my loyalty has to lie with the man who raised me. He gave me life, he gave me a home-- several homes, in fact. He has always made sure I had everything I needed, even if he's been more than a little distant all this time. On the other hand, Nikolai has saved my life twice now. He has put himself in harm's way to help me more than once, abandoning his own plans in the process. Surely, if there is anyone in this world I can rely on, it's him. But then… why would he want to hurt Daddy?

"Your father is not the typical businessman," he explains, pinching the bridge of his nose. "He's done much worse than fraud. He is responsible for the deaths of many people. Good people. Innocent people."

I grimace, my heart sinking. "Wh-what are you talking about?" I breathe.

He turns to look at me sorrowfully. "I don't want to have to tell you how evil your father is, Anastasia. Can't you just believe me?" he asks. Something about the way his voice sounds only breaks my heart even more.

But I shake my head. "No. You have to tell me. If you have a good reason, then say it. Spit it out. I need to know," I insist.

"Fine," he groans. "I won't beat around the bush. Your father is a high-ranking member of the Bratva. Do you know what that is?"

I frown and shrug. "No. What is it?"

"The Russian mafia," he says simply. My heart skips a beat.

"What?" I murmur, dumbfounded.

"Yes. That is the kind of business he runs. A criminal organization with strong ties to Moscow and to Brighton Beach. Why did you think he wanted you to marry Liev Ovechkin? It's not just because they are friends, Ana. It's a political alliance, an exchange of money and power for youth and beauty. Your body, your heart-- they're just assets for your father to bargain with. All this time, he's been grooming you into the perfect bride to be auctioned off to the highest bidder. How do you think your father met your mother?" he demands coldly.

My jaw drops. "What the hell are you implying?" I ask.

"Come on. You can figure it out, Ana. Your mother was bought and sold just like you're supposed to be. Your father purchased a young, beautiful woman to be his wife, to bear his child, and when he grew tired of her, he got rid of her. Collected a handsome chunk of insurance money in the process," he says.

I'm seeing red. My hands curl into fists as I start trembling. "No. You're wrong. My parents loved each other. My mom died when I was a toddler. She died in a car accident. Totally freak occurrence, nobody could've predicted it," I say, parroting the same story my father has always told me.

"Ever wonder why your father wasn't in the car with her?" Nikolai quips.

I throw up my arms angrily. "Who cares? They didn't go everywhere together! MY dad works a lot. That doesn't mean anything."

"It's not just your mother, either. Ana, your father is responsible for my parents' deaths, too," he adds. "You know why? Because they could not pay their debts. They were penniless and struggling to make ends meet, and indebted to the Bratva. So he made them pay with their lives. With my life, too. For years, I was an agent of the mafia, and not by choice."

"You're crazy. This is all a bunch of lies," I whisper, totally in shock.

Nikolai steps closer, pure sadness in those blue eyes. "Your father has hurt lots and lots of children, too. Young people trafficked for their bodies, their innocence sold to the highest bidder. That is the kind of business he runs. Nothing sells better than sex. That's why he is so successful, Anastasia. Nestor Koroleva is a bad man."

Tears rolls down my cheeks, and I feel my heart shattering into a million pieces. Nikolai isn't lying to me. I can tell. This is as hard for him to say as it is for me to hear. But it all makes sense. All the secrecy, the little hints adding up throughout the years. Clues that indicated that my father's business practices aren't above board. He's right. I know it.

But can I face the truth? Can I really watch as Nikolai destroys the one man who has been a constant fixture in my life since I was born? Can I let him take my father away from me?

Nikolai walks over to me slowly, his arms outstretched. I feel so worn out, so broken. I fold into his arms, my tears staining his shirt as he holds me close. I whimper and cry, letting the emotions overpower me. It's all too much, and I can't take it anymore. I need to think about something else, literally anything else. I need to be comforted. To be distracted. And this time, I know exactly how to get that.

I look up into my savior's face, imploring with my eyes.

He knows, too. He understands what I need.

*O*ur gaze lasts so long that it's painful. There is so much emotion flaring up in those defiant eyes of hers, so many wants and needs and questions. I am not so proud a man that I think I can assure a girl that everything is okay, even though she is coming to terms with the fact that her father is not the man she thought him to be a few days ago. But there is another kind of comfort I can provide, and I will provide it.

Because it's a comfort that both of us cannot resist giving each other.

I lean down and press my lips to hers. Her mouth is wet and hot, and with my hands on her back, I feel her every muscle start to relax. Slowly but surely, she melts into my grasp. What I am doing is wrong. I cannot deny that, and I don't want to lie and pretend this is something it isn't. Ours is no fairy tale romance. I am somewhere between this woman's captor and her savior, and I am sure she knows that. She is clever and cunning. There is more good sense in her than in her father. If all goes well, the things that mind of hers will be able to achieve can dwarf anything Nestor could ever do in New York City. But that is all in the future.

Right now, there is only me and Anastasia, basking in the warmth of each other's bodies.

I draw her body a little closer to me, and her stomach presses into the thick bulge in my pants. She feels my hardness, and she pushes herself closer into it with a soft moan. I can feel her every twitch. Her body is like a plaything in my hands, and I know just how she likes being played with. And I will never tire of her.

My tongue dives into her mouth, and she invites me in with hers. They dance together, feeling each other up and getting to know the shape of the other like new lovers. Like us. When I finally break the kiss, it is slow and deliberate. Her long eyelashes flutter as she opens her big eyes to peer up at me. Her face is still red and flustered. Her heart is still pounding hard and quick. What is there that my words could do?

Compared to my actions, words are nothing.

I let my hands slide down to her hips, and I squeeze. There is something primal in the way it feels, my possessive hands on her curvy hips. I desire her more than anything I've ever desired in my life. Lust has reared its head in my body, and I know I won't be able to lock it away again. Not after this. Not after everything we have been through.

"Let me comfort you, Ana," I say in a low, husky tone. "Let me show you everything I want to show you."

"You're a killer," she says. The words should hurt me, but they only feel like the truth.

"Yes. And I want to be a killer for *you*, Ana."

She stares at me a long time as we stand there together, our bodies perfectly still. We seem to move little, but we're weaving a careful dance together, trying to read one another's body language in each other's hands. And every word I said was true. I cannot lie to Ana. I know that now. I have the capacity to, but none of the will. She deserves far better than that. If there is anyone who deserves the power my honed body wields, it is Anastasia.

"Do I want a killer?" she asks, as if she can read my mind. I can't help but let a smile touch my lips. She is so small and fragile in my hands, but there is such power to her words. She has power she doesn't know what to do with, power that is undisciplined and wild.

"You know the answer to that," I say. Slowly, I release her, but I bring my hands to my own shirt. Just as slowly, I take hold of the hem and bring it up and over my shoulders before tossing it to the ground, leaving me bare-chested before her. I take her hands and put them on my pecs, and just like the first time we were naked together, she runs her hands over me, grazing them with her nails and feeling how rock-hard my body is.

"Is a good body supposed to convince me to let you kill my own father?" she asks after taking her time enjoying my chest.

"Not my body," I say. "But my mind. You know what I can do with all this, flesh and bones," I say, looking down at myself. "I am powerful, Ana, but I have purpose. And you are more deserving to wield it like a weapon than anyone I've ever met in the bratva."

"That's a lie," she says, though a smile plays across her face.

I take her chin in my hand and turn her face up to look at me. I give her a deadly serious glare, a glare that paralyzes her and makes her heart pick up speed again.

"If I wanted to lie to you, Anastasia," my voice rumbles, "we would never even be here to begin with." As I say the words, I reach down and grab her shirt. Before she can resist, I lift it up over her head and toss it aside. I reach around her for the hook of her bra, but she puts her hands up to stop my powerful arms. I freeze, watching her steadily, and we lock eyes.

"You like testing me," I say. "You enjoy my power."

I push my hands past her and unhook her bra, and before she can react, I walk her back to the wall, pinning her between it and me. I rip her bra off and discard it, leaving her as exposed as I am. She squirms, but I push her hand away and cover her breast with my hand. I squeeze, feeling its softness with my rough palm, toying with her nipple between my fingers. I pinch it and flick it, and she blushes, twisting left and right while I hold her still. I reach up and weave my fingers into her hair, taking a fistful of it and tilting her head back just enough to expose her neck.

My teeth go to her skin, and I ravish the flesh. I act as if I'm going to sink my teeth into her. Something primal inside me does. My left hand holds her hair while my right fondles her breast, and she soon lets her body relax while I have my way with her. I press the bulge of my crotch up against her stomach and grind against her. With each thrust, my cock pulses with an almost lazy, careless need, pure and unrestrained lust for the stunningly gorgeous woman in my grasp.

"I can do whatever I want with you," I growl into her ear, and I feel her whole body shiver. "You are mine, Ana, and I want to offer you everything my body can do."

"You don't know me," she breathes back.

"But I know what's best for you."

"Then show me."

The challenge in her voice makes my whole body feel more alive than it has in years. I pull her hair back more, making her eyes spring open. Our height difference is so great that I can look down at her with my head resting against the wall while she cranes her neck to look up at me, that bratty pout on her lips making my balls ache with need to release on her.

I smile.

"You are more of a bratva leader than you could possibly guess, little princess," I say.

I pick her up in my arms without warning and walk her to the couch, laying her down on it and looming over her. I kiss her, and she writhes and melts into it. My body covers her like a blanket, and my hands explore her freely. My kisses pepper her face, then make their way down to her neck and her collarbone. All the while, I feel her body, and soon, I'm working her pants off her. Finally, she is naked under me, nothing but her soft, vulnerable body to be ravished by my unrestrained hardness.

My mouth goes to her breasts, and I take my time with them, slowly moving my tongue around the swollen nipples and the pink areolas that need my attention so desperately. I get to know her breasts intimately.

As I bring my kissing lips down the center of her

breasts across her stomach and closer to that golden meeting point, her gasps and soft moaning fills my ears like sweet music from heaven. My whole body is desperate for her, and the pleasure she gets from my savage touch is enough to keep me burning forever.

My lips get to her lower ones, and I press my mouth to her and let out a rumble that makes her shiver with anticipation.

"I can smell your desire," I say. "You want me."

"I need you," she says. "I've needed you since you first held me."

"Good," I say. "I'm not going to let go."

Before she can reply, I stroke her pussy with my tongue. It goes from the bottom of her tight pussy up to the clit, and I hold nothing back. I stroke over and into her again and again, feeling how hot and wet she already is. She pushes her hips up into me, once, and I put my strong hands on her hips to hold her down and let me have my fun undisturbed. My tongue flicks out over and over again, striking the same rhythmic points as if I'm a musician with her as my instrument.

My eyes are closed, and I can feel every part of her folds in intimate detail. No matter how wet she is, I can feel every part of her. The way her clit swells as I tease it is familiar to me. It makes me want to have some part of her to grind against so that I can share in a fraction of the delight she's getting from my attention. Just like the first time, she runs her hands through my hair, but this time, it's not just for support. She has gotten to know my body, too.

While I pleasure her, her hands rove down to my muscular shoulders, then to my biceps. She wants to feel her favorite parts of me, and I am more than happy to oblige. Her hands move back up to my head, then down again, and her breaths only get quicker and hotter with each lick. The tip of my tongue strikes her swollen, needy clit over and over again until I feel a familiar tension building up inside her. I can sense it, like a change in the air, the subtlest of scents reminding me that she's about to come.

I work relentlessly on her until I hear a sharp cry from those pouty lips, and I release her hips to slide my hands under her ass. I drink from her, pushing her closer up against my face as she comes. She can't squirm away from me. There is no escape from my torment.

She hasn't finished coming when I take my face away from her pussy, and without any further waiting, I sit up on the couch and grab her hips. She's surprised, but my body is so large and strong that I have no trouble lifting her up off the couch and seating her on my lap. Her naked ass sits on the bulge of my pants, and immediately, she tries to grind into me, breathing heavily.

"That's a good girl," I muse, rewarding her efforts

by bringing my hands up to her breasts. She faces away from me, and I take her from behind, groping her and peppering her neck with kisses, feeling her sweet-smelling hair against my face.

I bring a strong hand down to her pussy once again, and with two fingers, I feel her tormented, exhausted clit. She shivers again when I touch it, and I nip at her neck as I start moving my fingers in small circles on her clit. She is wet and only getting wetter. Her honey stains my pants, and I mean to get much more out of her before I am finished. My right hand gropes her breasts relentlessly while my left hand tends to her pussy, and once again, I hold nothing back. With my mouth, I nip at the soft skin of her neck, then up to her ear, taking the edge of it between my sharp teeth and teasing it mercilessly.

"You're *my* good girl," I growl into her ear as I touch her, and her mouth falls open. "I will tell you what is best for you, and I will work your body like an instrument. I will kill for you. I will protect you. And you will open yourself to me. Do you want that, Anastasia?"

"Like I've never wanted anything," she whimpers, and I hook my fingers under her pussy. She lets out a sigh of delight as I start to stroke her insides. The wet noises my fingers make inside her fill my ears, mixing with the sounds of her soft sighs. My rock-hard legs and abs hold her like steel, more comfortable than the most luxurious couch. In my hands, I can do anything with her. That was no empty boast. And I'm going to make her come over and over again.

She squirms in my grasp as my electrifying touch drives her wild, but she can only move if I permit it. I hold the reins, and the only way she could escape is if she begged me for it.

My fingers get faster and faster, never breaking their pace, always steady and precise. Soon, I start using both hands to touch her, one on her clit and the other feeling up her insides. Once again, I feel her whole body winding up, ready to release, and she arches her back and lets out a cry that could almost wake the neighbors. Her hands clench the couch, desperate to cling to absolutely anything.

She comes, and it's so strong that I can feel it in my fingers. She is so much wetter and hotter than she was just a few minutes ago, and I'm not anywhere near finished with her.

"Nikolai!" she cries out, passionate and unrestrained. "Nikolai, oh god!"

Slowly, I draw my fingers out of her pussy and bring them up to her lips. Obediently, she licks her honey off my fingers, moaning as she lets her lips slide over those fingers that have been so good to her. She whimpers when I take them back, and I stand up with her still in my arms, limp and so very spent.

"Think we're finished, girl?" I growl, carrying her

into the bedroom. "Hardly. I'm going to drain myself in you."

"I wouldn't want it any other way," she says in that thick, sleepy voice that makes my cock stiff as a pillar. I toss her onto the bed, and she bounces, stretching out her beautiful limbs on the sheets as I pull my pants off and leave them behind, approaching her like a predator glaring down at the most delicious prey he has ever laid eyes on.

I don't even kneel on the bed with her. With savage energy, I grab her sensitive thighs with possessive, rough hands, and I drag her closer to me, smiling ominously.

I part her thighs and let her look at the sight of my spear looming over her, heavy balls swollen with need under her.

"You don't yet understand what it means that you are *mine*, Ana," I growl.

I penetrate her down to the hilt, and she lets out a sharp gasp of pleasure. Her tight pussy is soaking wet and so slick that it feels like my cock is gliding through pure honey all the way in, and my balls hit her ass with a wet slap as I pull her closer into me.

My hips start bucking into her, but this time, her eyes are wide open and gazing with pure lust up at my endless muscles as I pleasure myself with her body. I want her to know what it means to be used, what it means to be in the hands of a dominant man who can treat her right, guide her and strengthen her. My cock is thicker than it was when we were first together, because this time, I want this purely for her.

I feel every inch of her soft, hot pussy as I start bucking back and forth like a piston. My body is as precise as a machine and many times more deadly, but with her, I am so delicate that I won't harm her. I know her body so well already, despite our only having been together a few days. I feel as if we were made for each other, made to find each other's limits and caress them as a lover should.

The word *lover* carries so much more weight now. I seem to see the world in brighter colors when I am around Anastasia. Even as the world burns around us, even as I force her to accept the fact that I must slay her father, I feel the closeness that builds between us and threatens to swallow us like an ocean of bliss.

I welcome it. I crave it. I need it. I need *her*.

The crown of my bulging shaft is leaking precum and grinding against every surface it can find, deep inside her pussy. I am the master of her folds, and my rhythmic pistoning into her soft, most intimate of places is living proof of that.

I don't let myself hold back, just like every other action I have taken tonight. My hands grip her ass and feel up every bit of its roundness that I desire, my eyes ravish her naked form, and my cock fills up all the space she has to offer between her legs.

"I want you to say it, Ana," I growl in a husky tone. "Tell me that you are mine."

"I…" she gasps, but my relentless fucking makes it hard to even focus her words. The poor thing moves her lips, trying to speak, but each time she starts to get something out, my thick shaft thrusts deeper into her and makes her dizzy with overwhelming sensations. "I…I'm yours, Nikolai!"

"And I am yours, Ana," I growl, and just like that, I feel her pussy clench and well up with utmost need as she begins to come. She lets out a sharp cry that pierces the room as she comes, and I release all my restraints. My balls clench up, my shaft stiffens and loses its regular rhythm, and the next thing I know, everything is a white-hot blur of animalistic, savage fucking. I put a knee on the bed as they start to go weak, her power is so strong. Back and forth, I spill over the edge of the last bit of control I have over myself.

The next second, my pearly-white seed fills her up, shot after shot of hot, heady seed. I empty more into her than I thought possible, all while her body writhes and twists with her full-body orgasm.

After a golden minute, it is over, and we are left panting in the bedroom. Still stiff as a rock, I slide out of her, and the last few drops of my virile, white seed fall out onto her puffy, swollen lips.

Ana is defeated, nothing more than a quivering mess on the bed, breathing slowly and steadily. I pick her up and tuck her into bed on the other side of me before climbing in across from her. In the sheets, she finally opens her eyes and looks at me with overflowing love, and I feel her soft hand on my still-stiff cock.

No words pass between us. We don't need to say a thing. I have given her the comfort she so desperately needed, and I know now more than ever that I was right to put my faith in her. The future ahead of us is uncertain, but we will face it together. I know it.

It isn't long before a heavy sleep overtakes us. Even I am surprised by how fast and heavy it comes on, but it is the most restful sleep I have had in as long as I can remember.

And when dawn breaks and my eyes open...her side of the bed is empty.

I sit bolt upright, looking around. No light in the bathroom. No sounds from the kitchen.

I toss the sheets off me and head into the living room, and my jaw clenches at what I see. All her clothes are gone.

Ana is gone.

ANASTASIA

*J*came here expecting to confront my father. To tell him I know what he's done and I know what kind of an evil man he is. I know everything. Or at least, I suspect everything. When I woke up this morning just before dawn, I was still exhausted from the night before. The revelation, the fight, the make-up sex to distract me from my pain. This morning, I woke up a different woman. Less innocent, more determined. I'm resigned to my fate as the daughter of a terrible man. But there's still this tiny shred of me that doesn't believe it, or at least does not want to believe it. Until I can see the proof with my own two eyes, I can't just give up and offer my father up for the execution.

He at least deserves a chance to explain himself. And if there's nothing else I have learned from my father, it's that loyalty is tantamount to godliness. Our family may be small, it may be shattered into pieces. It may be unconventional, even hideous to look at. But it's still my family: my father and I, two moving pieces on the chessboard. He's the king, but I am the queen, and I am the one with the power here. That's why I sneaked out of bed this morning, careful not to wake Nikolai, and I crept out of the house, still wearing the same dress as yesterday. I quietly walked out of the tract home safehouse and left. It was so quiet, so empty. The development project has long since been abandoned for lack of funding, which is why the safehouse is such a secure location. Who would ever want to go there? It's just a row of identical, boring, beige block houses, half-finished and utterly without charm or value. The neighborhood itself is out in the middle of nowhere, the first pitiful steps toward establishing a new suburb that could be filled with happy, smiling families. Mothers jogging in the morning, pushing their baby strollers. Dads watering the lawn, waving to the neighbors. Kids playing pick-up basketball in the streets, safe in the knowledge that everyone around them only wants what's best for them.

Domestic paradise. A little monotonous maybe, but still a pretty picture of the elusive, ever-shifting American dream. But the money fell through before the dream could even spread its wings, and now the safehouse sits in relative obscurity out in the New York nothingness.

Luckily, though, I was able to get cell service. I walked to the end of the row of empty block houses, looked back to make sure Nikolai hadn't caught on and started following me, and I called a cab. My credit card account may be frozen, but I was smart enough to open my own account a while back. About a year ago, I got tired of having to show my father's credit card every time I wanted something. So I secretly opened a checking account. I sold a bunch of my old designer handbags and shoes on the internet, put the money in the account, and got a debit card in my own name. It has no attachment to my father. I only did it out of pride, but I am seeing now the benefits of being more independent.

At first, the cabbie didn't want to drive all the way out to the middle of nowhere to come collect me, but I offered him three hundred dollars and he changed his tune. The cab took about a half hour to reach me, and I spent those thirty minutes in a state of pure turmoil and anxiety, looking back over my shoulder, expecting Nikolai to wake up and realize I was gone. But he never came for me. Whether he was simply asleep or had given up on me, I still don't know. But now, it doesn't matter, because the cab driver took me all the way to Sands Point. To the mansion that I once called home, even though I rarely spent much time there. I had no way of knowing whether my father would be here or not. If he was here, the plan was to confront him in person, to ask him to answer to the same unbelievable accusations Nikolai hurled at him. I know my father better than anyone else, or at least I think I do. Surely I would be able to read his facial cues, his body language, to determine whether or not he was telling the truth.

And if he told me the truth, if the accusations were false, I was going to make the most difficult decision of my life. I was going to tell him about Nikolai's plan, to warn him that a very angry, very strong, very capable hitman was coming for him.

I was going to betray Nikolai.

But now that I'm here, standing in front of the home that isn't really a home, I can see that my father's beloved mint-green Aston Martin isn't parked in the circular driveway. The lights are out in the windows. Nobody is home. Well, except for me.

I stroll up the driveway to the front steps with a pit in my stomach. I wasn't expecting to find the place empty. But I suppose that makes sense. Anytime I expect my father to be around, he's missing. Every time I think I can count on him to be there for me, he's gone. For all I know he's over at the Ovechkin mansion, trying to appease his business partner and assure him that he'll find a way to drag me back, kicking and screaming, to the altar. Or maybe he's wandering around the state, looking for me. Who knows? And honestly, it doesn't matter. I can sit here and wait for him to come back.

I punch in the entry code to the front door, then press my thumb against the receptor to authorize the the door unlocking. I hold my breath, worried for a moment that maybe my father would have gone the extra mile and removed my prints from the authorization list as well as cutting off my credit card. I wait patiently, my heart hammering away in my chest, and then to my relief the robotic female voice (which I despise) chirps, "Entry unlocked. Welcome home."

I hear the electronic locks disengage in a series of clicks, and then I turn the knob and step inside. Immediately, my senses are flooded with waves of nostalgia. There is a familiar but indescribable smell to one's home that is instantly recognizable. It takes me back, reminding me of the brief but poignant moments I have spent in this house. Mostly for holidays or as a landing place in between trips to other countries or semesters abroad at boarding school. It occurs to me that it's totally possible my father still has some of the staff members present here. That could interfere with my plans, or at least make the confrontation with my father more awkward.

Taking a few steps into the foyer, I call out, "Hello? Is anyone here?"

I listen closely for a few moments, but all I get is silence, and the faint echo of my voice in the massive empty house. It's weird, seeing my home so devoid of activity. Usually there's at least a maid or a chef hanging around here, even when we have no intention of spending time here at all ourselves. My father has always been a stickler for cleanliness, and he orders the house to be cleaned constantly, whether we're expecting to stay here or not. But then again, I suppose maybe my father has other, more pressing concerns at the moment. Namely, trying to track me down so he can sell me off to Liev Ovechkin.

My steps echo as I walk into the living room, looking around for... who knows what. I wonder how long I'll have to wait here for him to return. It could take minutes, hours, or even days. I don't have days to waste on this fiasco. By now, Nikolai has surely realized that I'm missing, and he will make the only inference one could draw from my absence: that I've switched sides. That I've decided to turn away from the man who saved me, who derailed all his best-laid plans to look after me in a way my own father never has. I feel a pang of guilt in my heart at that thought. I don't feel good about leaving Nikolai. Especially after the passionate, amazing night we shared together. I'm still not sure I'm making the right choice. But I can't turn back now, can I? Nikolai is a hard man, and even though I can sense his soft spot for me, it would be foolish and self-absorbed of me to expect that he would continue trying to treat me with kid gloves now that I've so blatantly betrayed him.

I swallow hard. That is what I'm doing, isn't it? Betraying Nikolai. And if his accusations against my father are true, then I'm the one making a mistake here. But I can't just accept his version of reality as truth, not without hard proof or a confession. And since my father isn't here yet, I'll have to wait on that confession.

But then it occurs to me: maybe I can find proof.

Still questioning my own sanity, feeling endlessly guilty about betraying one man or the other, I start climbing the staircase up to the third floor, where my father's executive office is located. He had the third floor built specifically to house his office, wanting a totally separate space to work in. I never thought much of it, since it seemed only natural for him to want some kind of boundary between life and work. But now that I think about it, it seems kind of odd. After all, my father has always blurred the lines between work and life. He's never not on the clock to some degree. Yeah, he keeps it secret from me, but I've never nosed my way into his business before. I was always content to let sleeping dogs lie.

So what prompted the need for a separate space? Suddenly, that alone seems like a condemnation, proof that he's not the man I thought he was. I hurry up the stairs and down the hallway, stopping in front of the elegant mahogany doors so similar to the ones leading to Liev's office. I realize with a jolt that I have never been inside the room before. I never had a need to. There's an electronic code box at the door, just like at the entrance to the house. I bite my lip, wondering what the code might be. There's no place for a print-receptor, so it's got to be purely code-based. I wrack my brain for an answer. I type in my birthdate. It flashes red. Nope. That's not it. I try his birthday. Red again. I try my parents' wedding date. Again, red.

"Shit, what is it?" I mutter to myself.

On a weird hunch, I type in another date, and the light flashes green. My eyes go wide as my stomach twists uncomfortably. That's the right code. As I open the door, it hits me how horrific that is. The date that unlocks his office is my wedding date.

Which hasn't arrived yet.

That means he's been plotting my wedding date long enough to have made it his personal passcode to his office. This date is so important to him, so memorable, that he relies on it. That indicates to me that he's been planning this since long before he told me about it about a week ago. It's not the last-minute thing I thought it was. It's been in the works for a long time. Maybe even years. That does not bode well. If he's been able to keep my arranged marriage a secret for so long, what else could he be hiding from me?

I walk into the office with an invigorated sense of purpose. I'm not going to just wait around for Daddy to return. I'm not going to give him the courtesy of answering to his crimes face to face. I'm going to find proof that will either exonerate him or condemn him, and I'm not going to hold back. This time, I won't shy away from the truth, no matter how ugly it may be. I approach his desk and the first thing I see is a framed photograph of me as a toddler. At first, it almost melts my heart, but then I notice that the photograph is slightly warped, not lying flat in the frame. Like it's bent somehow. I pick up the frame and unscrew the cardboard back to withdraw the photo. To my surprise, it's a bigger picture than what can be seen at first. It's folded in half. I unfold it to see that it's actually a photo of my mother and me. My mom, beautiful and elegant even in a simply pair of jeans and a sweater, looks to be barely older than I am now. She's sitting on a couch-- the same brown leather couch downstairs-- looking down at me with such a warm look of pure love. I'm in a frilly pink dress, sitting on the floor with a big gap-toothed grin on my face. I must be about two or three. The date on the back says *May 2002.*

I pick the frame up to slide the photo back into it, but to my surprise, something else falls out the back of the frame. I frown and bend down to pick it up. I let out a gasp when I see that it's a tiny key. "What the hell?" I murmur to myself.

What does this go to? I look around the room, but at first I don't see an obvious answer. So I walk around to the other side of his desk and open up his laptop. Again, there's a passcode. I type in the wedding date again, and it works. "Shit," I breathe.

I sit down in the great leather armchair and begin to click on random files saved to his desktop. My father, for all his cleverness, has never been particularly tech-savvy. I'm sure he has no idea how to encrypt information or what have you. I open up a file named BLOOM LIST, remembering that the private airline rumored to carry trafficked underage children is called the Bloom Express. To my horror, I find a massive, almost endless spreadsheet with the names and photos of countless children, all of them wearing frightened expressions, some with tears visible in their eyes. There are categories marked: "date of acquisition" and "date of sale" along with an even more repugnant column labeled, "date of disposal." The dates go all the way back to the 1980s, two decades before I was born. I scroll down, too transfixed by panic to stop, and my heart does a painful thump when I see a familiar face, one that looks bizarrely like mine. Only this young girl has blue eyes, where I have brown.

"No," I murmur. "No, no, no." I check the name beside it.

Karina Petrekova.

My mother's name. "No!" I exclaim, my hands trembling as I move to close the file and back away from the computer with tears in my eyes. My mother was one of the trafficked girls. She was probably bought for my father as a gift or something unimaginable. My own mother! But then, before I can click the X to close out of the spreadsheet, curiosity overtakes me. I need to know. I verify that her date of acquisition and sale occur prior to my parents' wedding anniversary, and then I scroll over to check the date of disposal.

It's the date of her death. January 1, 2004. New Years Day. My father always told me that she was hit by a drunk driver returning home in the wee hours, after a long night of partying. But now I have more than enough information to make me suspect that story. After all, what kind of husband would have filed his wife's tragic death as a "date of disposal?"

I close the file and turn away, trying not to cry. I've seen enough. But just as I'm about to rush out of the room, I notice an ugly gray lockbox in the corner of the room, sitting on a bookshelf in between the novels. Holding the tiny key in my hand, I walk over and kneel down, my heart racing. I lift the key to the lock, and to my surprise, it fits. I turn it and hear a click, and the lockbox door swings open. Inside of it are several thick wads of cash, both in American dollars and in Russian rubles. Nestled neatly between them is a stack of leather-bound books. I pull them out and my jaw drops as I realize it's a pile of old passports. The first three all bear my father's photo, but with names I don't recognize. The fourth one belonged to my mother. In her photograph, she looks to be no older than I am now. The fifth and sixth bear names I don't recognize, but the faces... they look familiar. Especially the one with a man's photo.

The man looks a lot like Nikolai. Only the birth-date is 1964.

The answer hits me full in the face. This is Nikolai's father, and the other must be his mother. Nikolai was right. He has been telling the truth about my father, about the criminal enterprise he's been running right under my nose all these years. The man who raised me is not a good man. Quite the opposite... he's the devil. A wolf in sheep's clothing. And all this time, I have defended him. I have believed in him. I've trusted him.

I loved him.

I reach into the lockbox, feeling around for anything else. As long as I'm discovering the truth, I might as well learn as much as I can about the man who is swiftly turning into my enemy. If I'm going to back to Nikolai with this information and beg him to forgive me for doubting him, I don't want to go back empty-handed. I fumble around and find a sheet of paper covered in a thick layer of dust. I pull it out, blow off the dust, and start reading. It's a typed document with my father's signature at the bottom, and as I read over the legalese, it dawns on me that this is some kind of will. It looks pretty old, but it outlines the fact that in the case of my father's death, all of his estate, his earnings, his business ventures both legal and illegal, should pass on to me-- but only if I remain unmarried at the time of his death.

There is a clause that states that if or when I marry, all of my inheritance shall pass to my husband. "Oh my god," I whisper, horrified. No wonder Daddy has been so dead-set on marrying me off to Liev. He doesn't want me to take over the business. Liev is his partner in crime, and he wants to continue running the empire without me around to meddle in it. He wants to nullify my power, take away what I would have been granted.

If he dies before I marry Liev... it will all be mine. The money, the power, the reputation. Of course, I have never wanted that kind of power, and I certainly don't want his reputation. I refuse to be the criminal my father is. But if I inherit his estate, I could turn over a new leaf. I could use the power and the money and the influence for good. My heart is pounding so quickly that when I stand up, I nearly fall over with dizziness. It's so much to take in, so much to comprehend. I can't believe how wrong I have been all these years, how messed up it is that all this time I've been financially benefiting from the evil work my father has done.

I know I can't go back in time and change the past, but maybe, just maybe I can do something to change the future. I know what I have to do.

"**A**re you ready for this?" I ask, watching Ana as she holds the phone in her hands, sitting on the bed quietly. She is silent for a long time, but finally, she nods, looking up at me with resolution in her eyes.

"Yeah," she says. "I'm ready."

Our eyes are locked for a few long moments, and even after everything we have agreed to, there is tension in the air. I have no doubt that she can taste it just as well as I can.

"I will be listening," I say, nodding back to the living room where I have my laptop set up to monitor the call. "Remember, it's okay for you to be nervous. He will be expecting you to be. It might look more suspicious if you're enthusiastic."

"I know," she says. "I've played the part before. I don't think he knows I'm capable of lying."

I crack a smile, but it soon fades.

"I don't have to tell you that the situation is completely in your hands now," I say. She gives he a hard stare. She knows exactly what I'm talking about, even though we don't have to say anything.

If she wanted to, she could easily use this chance to rat me out to her father. I wonder whether she knows I wouldn't kill her. Regardless, she could abort everything in the next few minutes. Part of me doesn't want to trust her with this, but the rest of me knows it's the right thing to do. All I can do now is hope that she sees reason.

"Let's get this over with," she says, and I turn and leave the room, making my way over to the table in the living room where I settle down and put on my headphones to monitor the call that will make or break everything my comrades and I have worked for. Within seconds, I hear the phone ringing...then comes the voice of Nestor Koroleva.

"Anastasia," he says. His voice is cold.

"Daddy," Ana says, and I have to admit, I'm impressed by how broken she sounds. I can taste resignation in every syllable.

"What do you want, Anastasia?"

"I…"

"Finally deciding to see reason?" he asks.

"Daddy, please, I-"

"Don't waste my time, Anastasia," he says. "You've done enough damage as it is. I raised you better than to stammer. Now tell me, is your childish little fantasy coming to an end, or are you just taking up more of my time to act out again?"

I hear a pause for what sounds like genuine sniffling on Ana's part. Nestor is silent. He knows damn well what he's doing, picking at her ego to keep her from thinking she has the upper hand. He's a sharp man who is used to this evil business.

"I don't want to be away anymore, Daddy," she whimpers. "Are you sure I have to go through with this to come back?"

"You know the answer to that, girl," he says. "Now, are you ready to act like an adult and come to your senses?"

"...I hate you, Daddy."

"That's not an answer to my question."

"Fine," she says. "Where do I have to go?"

I carefully write down every relevant detail as Ana sets up arrangements with her father. The conversation lasts some time, but it's obvious to me that Nestor has been planning this for a long time. He has a clear plan for how things must happen, and it confirms my suspicions that the business ties between him and Liev go deeper than even I expected.

By the time the phone call is over, I have all the information I need.

Nestor has a private lodge upstate in the mountains. He'll have things ready in three days' time, probably because he worries that his daughter will try to back out again, so he wants things ready as quickly as possible. I was pleased to hear Ana bargain with him, making him agree for it to be as small a ceremony as possible.

The fewer people in attendance, the more likely it will be that every single person there deserves the fate that I'm preparing for them.

She also demanded that she not come to him until the day of the wedding. That was a much harder sell for Nestor--not unreasonably. Ana could easily make him look like a fool by preparing the wedding only for her not to show. But he didn't have much of a choice.

When Ana appears in the doorway, walking toward me, I stand up and smile at her as I cross the room to take her in my arms in a comforting embrace.

"You make a fine actress and negotiator," I say sincerely.

"I've never had to make a phone call like that in my life," she murmurs into my chest. "I don't know how I can even speak to him. That man...he's not who I thought he was. I can even hear his voice differently now."

I stroke Ana's hair and kiss her on the head, holding her snugly to me.

"You did better than I could have hoped," I say.

"What happens now?" she asks, turning her head up to look at me.

"Now, I put my plans into motion," I say. "And you do just a little more acting."

ICE CRUNCHES under even the most careful of steps, so I hold my body utterly still, crouching around the corner of the massive, snowy rooftop of the luxurious lodge.

The sound of footsteps draws closer. I ready myself, slowing my breath so that not even my visible breath in the chilly air of early springtime can give me away. Seconds pass like minutes until the guard making his way around the corner is right on top of me.

Silent as a shadow, I lurch upward, garroting wire in my hands, and I whip the thin string of metal around the man's neck. Before he can tense up, Maxym slips around from behind me and grabs the gun out of his hand while I strangle the man. Slowly, the guard's thrashing dies down, and he soon goes limp in my arms. Wordlessly, Maxym and I lay him down on the ground and move his gun away from him where it can't slide off the roof.

All around the building, my comrades are all doing the same thing, neutralizing the outside guards one by one. I give Maxym a nod, then proceed with him further down the roof to the point of entry we planned out.

We didn't even have to bribe one of the caterers to get us information about this lodge--Ana told me all I needed to know.

The three days between the phone call and now were tense. Ana nearly backed out more than once, but she stayed the course, and I rallied my men. All the prisoners who are here with me today are men who have been burned by the bratva over time, people like me who are only playing the bratva's games while they bide their time for the perfect moment.

A moment like this.

And now that we have the chance to strike, we aren't about to let it go to waste.

We already have confirmation that Nestor and Liev are present. Right about now, Liev's grooms-men--his toadies that worship him in the bratva-- are making their way down the aisle with him, waiting for Nestor to walk Ana down the aisle to give her away in just a few moments. Time is of the essence. This has to be perfectly coordinated.

Maxym watching my back, I make my way to the utility door and use a stolen key to unlock it, slipping inside. Maxym doesn't follow me until I'm a few paces ahead of him. He knows what the plan is.

I hurry down the narrow hallways surrounding the sweeping atrium in the lodge that is often used for conferences or business dinners. Ana had been here several times as a child, and she was able to tell me the basics of the layout. From there, it was just a matter of study.

After a short flight of stairs, I crack open a door leading to the outer hallway, and I move out when I see that the way is clear. My path takes me around the corner, and before I round it, I take out one of the silenced pistols from the holsters on my chest. I whip around the corner and see two guards standing at the doorway to the foyer.

Two quick shots is all it takes. They never even knew what killed them.

I slip into the foyer, and just like that, I see two figures standing about five feet from me with their backs to me, facing the doors leading to the ceremony proper.

One of the figures is Ana.

She is dressed in a large bridal gown, looking absolutely radiant. At the same time that I see her, the bridal music starts playing on an automated track over the speakers of the whole building. But I don't have time to linger on the sight of her. The man next to her is the one I'm after.

Nestor Koroleva.

As swiftly as I've entered the building and dealt with the guards, I sweep up behind Nestor as he steps through the open door with Ana in his arm.

The three of us appear before the wedding ceremony together.

Nestor freezes as he feels the barrel of the gun on the back of his head, and I hear a gasp ripple through the audience, followed by the sounds of a dozen guns cocking.

The scene is sublime.

Ana and Nestor stand frozen in front of me on the red carpet that leads down the room to where Liev and his men stand, staring at me with mouths hanging open in shock. The audience is barely an audience at all--just a few business friends of the two men, further showing how much of a business deal this really is. Ana is the only woman in the entire room. The sounds of guns cocking are from the interior guards, all of them training their weapons on me. The only reason I'm not dead is the fact that I have Nestor as my hostage now. All the while, the bridal march chimes overhead as if nothing has happened.

"You lost my invitation," I say, and Nestor tenses up. Ana says nothing, jaw tight, staring forward.

"*You*," Nestor hisses, and he turns his head enough to look at Ana. "Was this your doing, you brat? Is this who you've been running around with?"

"This is a lot longer coming than that, Daddy," she says in a pitiless tone.

The windows shatter.

All around the room, bullets fly in to strike the

guards as my army of ex-convicts bursts into the room from the windows, the rafters, the doors, every place they've made it to. Ana turns and runs behind me, right into Maxym's arms, as planned, and he guides her away from the firefight while I grab Nestor's neck and pull him in closer to me.

"You could have been something, you piece of shit," he snarls at me as he thrashes in my grasp.

"I am more than you'll ever be," I say, and I put a bullet in Koroleva's head.

He hasn't even hit the ground before I look up to see Liev already down, but still alive. He struggles for a weapon from one of the dead guards not far from him, but I fire a round that hits his hand, and he howls in pain, recoiling. The firefight is still happening all around me, but my men have the situation on lockdown. Most of the guards died in the first volley, and now, my men are entering the building, fighting with the survivors hand to hand and finishing off the other minions of these two monsters.

"To think I hated you for throwing a wrench in my plans, springing the marriage at the last minute," I say to Liev as I point my gun at him. "But I should be thanking you. Without Ana...your ends wouldn't have been nearly so dramatic."

"Eat sh-" he starts to spit, but I silence him with a single bullet to the head.

All around me, the sounds of death are like a

choir to my ears. I look around and see the architects of so much suffering meeting their just ends at the hands of the people they wronged. It is strange, I should feel more triumphant than any other moment in my life--this is what I've been working toward since I was forced to join the bratva. But now, all I can think about is what the other men are feeling, and it makes me swell with pride.

But that isn't the other thought on my mind.

I turn and head out the room to find Ana...and congratulate Maxym on the position I'm going to give him for his part in protecting her.

When the smoke finally clears, my men have suffered no casualties. The lodge is a mess of broken glass and blood, but every one of our enemies is accounted for. It was a flawless operation. While I tend to Ana, keeping her comforted and distracted from the ugly reality of the massacre, the men set to cleaning up the place.

That isn't all we do, either. We have to do something with the bodies, but thankfully, we planned for that. I have the bodies of the bosses and their men loaded onto that wretched, evil plane of theirs, as if they were just on their way from the wedding.

Maxym helps me rig the explosives on the thing so that it looks like an engine malfunction when it goes up in flames, destroying any shreds of evidence tying me to the massacre I orchestrated today.

I have conducted mass assassinations before, but never quite like this.

And this isn't even the end of it. My men and I are cleared out of the lodge by nightfall, and as soon as our business is tied up, Ana and I start blazing a path back down to Brighton Beach.

We have some diplomatic business to tend to.

"*A*na, are you ready?"

I look up at the sound of Nikolai's voice, slicing through the fog of anxiety surrounding my head like a storm cloud. The man I adore, my savior who caught me as I fell, the one who has shined the brightest light into my life to illuminate the foul secrets and filthy lies gathering up in the corners, stands in the doorway. He's wearing all black, an Armani suit specially designed and tailored to accentuate every smooth line and rounded muscle of his body. His inky-black hair is swept back away from his face, and he's freshly clean-shaven. He looks every bit the part of the enforcer, but with a touch of elegance I hope our new associates will be able to appreciate.

I'm dressed similarly, to create an impression of a

unified front. To indicate that he and I are a package deal, and we will work side by side to take charge of my father's post. I'm wearing a jet-black Dolce and Gabbana cocktail dress with a frilly tie-neck and tulle cap sleeves, along with Manolo Blahnik slingback pumps exactly the shade of blood. My lipstick is the same shade, as are my nails. My eyeliner wings are sharp as the blade of a paring knife, and my hair falls in shiny, vampy curls around my shoulders. It's quite the contrast to the casual, more summery style I usually wear, but there's a reason for the change. I need to ease into my new image. My new reputation. I can't face my associates wearing a yellow sundress and sandals, looking like some ditzy schoolgirl. I will never be my father, and I don't have any desire to fill his shoes the way he did, but I do have to impress the men I'm about to meet with. More than that, I have to make them respect me, if not trust me. I don't expect them to like me, but they had better accept me as their new leader.

Part of revamping my image and reputation has more to do with how I feel, though, rather than how I look. I am still reeling from the loss of my father. It's only natural to grieve for him, or rather, the idea of him I built up in my head. All those years, I trusted him and loved him just as any loyal daughter regards her doting father. But the version of him I adored was just an illusion. A mirage in the desert arising from the dusty expanse out of intense loneliness. He played the game like an expert. Daddy knew just how to keep me on his side. He knew how to isolate me, to keep me cornered and alone in the world. If I didn't have any other friends or family to rely on, I would be forced to depend entirely on him. He was my only contact, and I saw the world through whichever false filter he held over my eyes. He tricked me into believing his lies and never questioning his logic, intentions, or authority. Everything he did for me was part of an overarching contrived effort to keep me in the dark, almost to brainwash me. He needed to control me so that I could never gather the strength and know-how to defy him.

I wonder when he began to suspect I might be trouble. I wonder if he ever expected that at all. My gut tells me that Daddy never really put much thought into what kind of woman I would grow up to become. I was always just an investment to him, another asset along with his vacation homes and his stock market value. He underestimated me, down to the very end. He never saw it coming, not from me, his precious, sheltered little angel.

Hell, before Nikolai came into my life, I never saw it coming, either. I always knew I was smart and capable, but my father had me so distracted with luxury and travel that I rarely got the opportunity to prove my worth. All my dreams of growing up and finding my place in the world, not following in my father's footsteps as a businesswoman, but blazing my own path to do good things in the world, to set things right, seemed to disappear when I was engaged to Liev Ovechkin. Good old Uncle Liev never suspected me, either. The two men would have laughed their asses off at the suggestion that I might have more going on in my head than just a pretty face. And judging by the way they and men like them treat women, it's no surprise. In their world, women are just shiny toys to pass around and dispose of when you get tired of playing with them. That's what the Bloom Express group have done with children and women for over two decades. That's what my father did with my beautiful, good-hearted mother.

She was disposable to him. But not to me. I know that, had she been given the chance to live, to truly bloom as her own person, she would have been incredible. She was cut down before she got the chance to shine. But not me. And what happened to her will never happen again to another woman or child, not on my watch. It will be an adjustment period for my new associates, of course, but they will have to get over it. Because we are never going back to the way things were before. I'm better than that. Nikolai is better than that. And together? We're unstoppable.

I'm sitting in the big leather armchair behind my

father's old mahogany desk in his spacious private office in our Sands Point home. After he died, I was of half a mind to tear the whole place down. Just raze it to the ground and rid myself of all the tainted memories. But I realized that was the easy way out. I don't have to obliterate those memories. I just have to take what I have and make it work. I have to take straw and spin it into gold. So we cleaned out the office, gathering up all the incriminating evidence of my father's evildoing and filing them away in a safehouse. He's already dead, so no use handing it over to the police just yet. We tidied up the house and I settled into the office, still weighed down by dark memories and shame. It's a heavy burden to bear and a massive undertaking for anyone, but I can do it. With Nikolai's support, I can do damn near anything.

I give Nikolai a nod. "Yes. I'm ready. Send them in," I tell him softly.

He smiles at me, one of those gorgeous blue eyes closing in a wink. With Nikolai at my side, we can handle anything. He makes me strong. He makes me fearless. He makes me realize the scope of my own worth. I'm much smarter and tougher than Daddy ever thought I could be, and now it's the moment of truth. It's time to prove myself. It's time to usher in a new era.

Nikolai opens the door and beckons for the seven men to walk into my office. They are all similarly dressed in dark clothing and grim expressions. Their wrists are adorned with shiny metal Rolexes, their chests gleaming with gold chains. Even the buttons of their suit jackets are carved from expensive ivory, pearl, and opal. These seven men form the most elite upper echelon of the Brighton Beach chapter of the Bratva.

Well, the most elite besides Nikolai and me.

The men file into the room with obvious reluctance, and I know without having to think about it at all that all of them are armed. That's fine. I expect that. After the gruesome deaths of my father and Ovechkin, they must all be on edge. Whose neck will be on the chopping block next? What kind of trap could they be walking into right now? But the point of this meeting is to put those fears to rest while simultaneously assuring them that I am in charge, and I will not accept disobedience. Nikolai closes the door behind them and I stand up to greet the group with a gracious smile, leaning forward on my father's old desk.

"Good afternoon, gentlemen," I say pleasantly. "You all look well."

None of them say a word. I could hear a pin drop in this room. They're all waiting on me.

"Right. I see no reason to beat around the bush, so I'll cut straight to the point. I'm sure you have all come here today carrying your own unique prejudices, assumptions, and motivations. I don't blame you. Any time there is a shift in the power dynamics of a long-established group such as this one, there are bound to be some growing pains. And some dissenters," I begin, making sure to hold eye contact with each one of them in turn.

Again, they remain silent. That's fine by me.

I continue with a smile. "Now, I don't know exactly what your individual roles are in regards to how my father, the late Nestor Koroleva, used to run things. As you can probably guess, he kept a lot of secrets from me. He never wanted me to inherit this role. He never expected me to take his place. Despite all of his careful planning, he never quite considered the possibility that I might be a living, breathing, thinking human with agency and opinions. I lived in his blind spot. A pity for him, I suppose, but an advantage for me. Because now I have legal control over his estate. All of his money and influence are mine. That also means that all of his sins weigh down on my shoulders. I know you have all played your own important role in those sins. God only knows how many children, how many women, you all have hurt. Killed. Treated like chattel. But not anymore.

"My father's death and his legacy cast a long, oppressive shadow over me, but it's my plan today to start inching my way out from underneath it to stand in the light. Nestor Koroleva was a bad man. A criminal, not just against the law of the land, but against humanity itself. I seek to undo those crimes. I can't take back all the years of pain he has inflicted upon the world in his selfish pursuit of money and power, but what I can do is point this organization in a different, brighter direction for the future. We will no longer be agents of harm, but of mercy. We will suck out the poison. We will right the wrongs. And you all will do so, as well, as loyal and devoted members of the family.

"Now, I must warn you. Just because I have good intentions does not mean I didn't also inherit some of my father's more-- ahh, aggressive tendencies. Just like him, I require fidelity. I require honesty. I demand respect, though I also plan to earn it. We will continue to prosper, but not on the backs of those we make to suffer for our own selfish gain. Not anymore. If you came here today expecting me to follow in my father's footsteps, you are mistaken. But if you think for one second I will not deal with objectors with the same ruthlessness that he did, you are wrong again. My partner is a formidable enemy, and so am I. Do not test my patience. I want to reign with cooperation and compassion, but if you betray me or my vision, I won't hesitate to cut you down. You will be buried along with my father and Ovechkin, and I will not mourn for you.

"That said, I want you all to be able to trust me. I will never lie to you. I am doing the right thing. I'm not a tyrant-- I am a diplomat. I have lopped off the head of the beast, but I know a coup like this can sew the seeds of vengeance and rebellion. I will watch you all closely to see how well you can fit into this new era. We are going to face the light again. We are going to use our money and control to do good things for once. Take this opportunity I'm offering you to atone for your sins. This is an olive branch. This is a second chance. Let's move forward together into the light," I conclude.

There's silence for a moment and I make eye contact with Nikolai, who gives me a slight nod of approval. Then, one of the men speaks up and says, "And why should we accept your rule? We have never had a diplomat-- or a woman, for that matter-- at the helm. How can you possibly expect us to just fall in line with your ideas that differ so much from your father's?"

A slow, wry smile spreads across my face as I stand up straight, staring at him unblinkingly. The other man shift awkwardly, not knowing what to say.

"Look around," I answer cheerfully, "have you noticed how clean and empty my father's old office is now?"

The men all look around, confused. The one who spoke up says, "Yes. We all know you're capable of cleaning house. You are a woman, after all."

Emboldened by his crude statement, a low titter of laughter rolls through the group. I remain patient and composed, even though I can sense that Nikolai has a little more trouble keeping his true feelings at bay. Once the silence resumes, I explain, "This room used to be filled with all sorts of evidence. Files, folders, letters, emails, spreadsheets, a lockbox-- all sorts of items that could be very, very interesting to the police. My father was an arrogant man. He got complacent. This office was a treasure trove of evidence, implicating not only himself and Liev Ovechkin, but every single one of you, as well. But me? I am much, much more organized. Like you said, I'm a woman. And I know that everything should be in its place. All of that evidence, reaching back nearly three decades, is now housed in a secure, secret location only Nikolai and I know about. You see, I don't need a gun to keep you all in line. All it would take is one call to the mayor of New York City, with whom I have cultivated a very good friendship over the years, and every single one of you would be thrown behind bars for so long you will never feel the warmth of the sun on your skin ever again."

All around the room, there's a faint sigh of defeat. I'm not bluffing, either. I attended boarding school with the mayor's granddaughter for several years. After some quick, efficient diplomacy, I have the mayor's personal cell on speed dial. And from the looks of resignation on the faces of my associates, they know I'm telling the truth.

"Well, I think that's more than enough for our first meeting. It's been a pleasure doing business with you all," I say brightly. "You're dismissed. Have a wonderful afternoon. Oh, and boys? Watch your backs."

In the dead of night, I return to our penthouse that overlooks the water pulling my sleek black car into the driveway and stepping into the elevator that takes me up the many floors to my love.

My muscles are still relaxing from the thrill of the job. It has been a long night, but it never wears on me anymore like it used to. Now, I feel that every step I take is in the right direction.

I am a killer. That much will never change.

But now, I'm killing for her.

I unlock our door and step inside, listening to the bolt locks click into place behind me as I step into the dark room.

"Is it done?" a voice asks me, a voice sweeter than honey and more delicate than fresh snow--Ana's voice. I look up to see her silhouette lounging on the couch, and I flick the light on to see her reclining with a glass of white wine in her hand, smiling up at me with those full lips, her soft figure still wearing the evening gown she wore to some dinner or other for business this evening.

It has been a busy few weeks, solidifying her place at the top of the food chain in Brighton Beach's bratva. But Ana is a natural, whether she wants to admit it or not. And the more she grows into her new role, the more she seems to know it, at least privately.

"Quickly and quietly," I say, "as always. A single shot to the head while on his yacht. I saw him hit the ground before I left the scene. I was seen by no one."

Her face melts into a genuine smile.

"It's over, then? That was the last of them?"

"There are no other Ovechkin loyalists holding out against you," I say, "as far as I know, at least. We should stay sharp, as always."

"I would expect nothing less from you," she purrs as I approach her and loom over her form sprawled on the couch. "But that doesn't mean we can't celebrate."

"Is that an order, madam?" I ask, smiling as I start to strip my jacket off and toss it aside, feeling my cock swelling already at the sight of my love.

"I think I've had my fill of giving orders today," she says, stretching out, and before she can even finish the action, I scoop her up into my arms and lift her up effortlessly. She slides her hands around the back of my neck and pulls herself up to kiss me while I carry her to the bedroom, feeling my heart pound harder for my girl.

"You're right," I growl before I set her on the bed and straddle her without another moment's preparation. "Let's take some of that control out of your hands, shall we?"

She squirms under my legs, and I reach down to stroke her hair with these large, powerful hands of mine--hands that have killed very recently.

I have spent the past few weeks taking care of all of our enemies--all of Ana's enemies, now that she is taking control of the power structure her father risked destroying for so many years. Together, we will run New York City better than any of those old monsters ever could. As long as my body serves me, I will be her muscle, and she will be the face of a brighter future than we could ever hope for.

I bend down and kiss those soft, pouting lips that I fell in love with at first sight, and I their warmth fills me as she puts a hand to my face and strokes it. It trails down to my body, and she tugs at my shirt, silently begging me to take it off.

I oblige, sliding the fabric over my head and behind me before I take off my belt, watching her with a cruel smile. I take her wrists as she watches me carefully, and I tie her hands to the headboard, restraining her gently yet firmly. Once that's done, I reach over to the nightstand and slide it open, taking out a small strip of black silk.

"I wanted to make you mine from the moment I saw you, Ana," I say, "but I never thought you would hold these kinds of tastes in that innocent heart of yours."

I blindfold Ana while a smile curls her lip up, and she laughs softly.

"Nothing I'd entertain if it weren't for you," she says, a blush coming to her lips. "It flashed in my mind when we saw each other first. You had this kind of...*energy* around you. I wanted it. I wanted you to take me somewhere private and claim me while we still had our clothes on, Nikolai."

The thought makes my cock twitch in my pants, and I unbutton them, letting my shaft spring forth and feel the cool air of our apartment as I glower down at my captive woman. My big hand goes to my cock and strokes it thoughtfully as I growl.

"If you knew half the things I wanted to do to you when we first saw each other," I say in a husky tone, "you would fear me, my love."

"I already fear you," she breathes. "And I love every second of it."

My hands run up and down her body, feeling the expensive fabric of her dress and grasping her figure, feeling my body get hungrier for her with each passing moment. Neither of us want to wait around. Sometimes, her needs are savage and rough, and I am here for all of them.

I lift her legs up and reach up under her dress with savage ferocity, and I feel the heat of her puffy, swollen lips through her thin panties. My heart pounds fiercely as I pull the thin fabric aside and pull her closer to me.

I slide my cock into her lips, past her underwear, and I feel her wet heat envelop my bulging, dark crown. Her whole body shivers as I awaken it, penetrating her with my own hot shaft and feeling every inch of space she has to offer between her legs. I grab her hips and buck into her all the way to the hilt, possessively filling up my girl with me.

My rough hands push her dress up around her waist, and my fingers dig into her as I start rutting hard and fast. The thrill of a completed job is still pulsing through my veins with every heartbeat that makes me cock swell up thick and hard inside Ana, and she needs to unwind from a long, stressful day. For once, we have no desire for foreplay, no need to draw things out long and slow.

Sometimes, going hard and fast is exactly what one needs.

For me and Ana, that is how our relationship started. We were impulsive, brazen, nearly throwing all our plans to the wind to make it happen. But together, we have prevailed, acting on pure instinct and raw need.

Why change perfection?

My hips start bucking into my bound and blind-folded lover, thrusting up into her with more force every time. She knows me and how my cock feels, what it needs, and exactly how to pleasure me the way I want while I give her more than she ever dreamed of. I feel the tip of my cock push through her wet folds and glide as deep as it can go before I bring it back out, almost far enough to leave her entirely, then drive myself back in again.

I rock back and forth, gaining speed each time I pound into her. I'm still wearing most of the clothes I wore on the job. The smell of my car is still on me.

"These are the hands of a killer, Ana," I growl as I dig my fingers into her hips. "And for you, I will turn them on anyone you wish."

"Don't hold back," she begs me in that soft, whimpering tone that drives me crazy. Despite growing into her strong, domineering role in busi-ness, she still wants me to take the reins in bed, still begs me for control, to show her more power than she knows how to handle. She is still the innocent girl I rescued from that monster in the manor. It feels like a lifetime ago, even though it has barely been a month.

I lift her left leg up and drape it over my shoulder so I can take her sideways, and the new sensations make her gasp and dig her teeth into her lip, strug-gling against her restraints. Her hands claw for something to hold onto, but the belt keeps her from doing so. She is mine, and I can subject her to anything I want.

I reach down with one hand and grope her breasts, feeling their firmness through her clothes as I pound into her. My hips are like a piston, relentless and precise, never losing energy or speed for so much as a moment. She likes it rough and hard, and that's exactly how I give it to her.

My stubble brushes across her smooth leg as I kiss her thigh while pounding into her. I feel her getting tighter by the moment, and soon, her face is blushing and her pussy is getting wetter, like a string ready to be plucked.

She's coming, and that makes me swell all the harder. I have to hold myself back at all times when inside her. She has an effect on me like no other woman, and I want to reward her for that.

Finally, I feel her insides pulse and contract, and she whimpers delightedly as her first orgasm rolls through her body like waves of electricity sending relaxation from her lower abdomen all throughout her body. I never thought of myself as a man who could deal in life as well as death, but when I look at the way my cock makes Anastasia feel, I know it to be who I truly am.

I am a provider for her in more ways than one.

Once her orgasm comes to an end, I push myself forward as far as I can go and bend down to kiss her soft lips, then bring my mouth to her neck to ravish the soft skin while I undo her bindings for a moment.

"Remember our safety word," I say in a low, husky tone as I pick her up and turn her around on the bed so that she faces away from me on her knees.

"Sedan," she repeats, nodding.

"Good girl," I say, and I slap her on the ass with a sharp crack. She shivers and smiles, bending over to present her ass to me. I grab her wrists and use my belt to tie them behind her back, leaving her again restrained before me. She looks so beautiful, kneeling before me in an evening gown that's getting more fucked up with every passing minute I have to claim her.

If it gets ripped, it won't be the first, and it won't be the last.

From behind, her panties are more of a problem that I don't feel like tangling with. I take the thin, expensive fabric from behind and rip it with a quick, hard gesture, and I toss the torn cloth behind us before groping her ass and perching my cock on her lips, holding it there without diving in.

I take a moment to enjoy her round ass, feeling how smooth and supple her flesh is, taking my time groping it possessively.

"Do you like it?" she asks, still panting from the exertion of getting fucked relentlessly.

"Everything about you, Ana," I say, "is exquisite.

And it is *mine*," I growl. As I speak, I spear her with my cock, and it twitches at the sound of her delighted gasp as I fill her up, grinding against her g-spot before getting right back to the same rhythm I was pounding her at earlier. But this time, the angle lets me reach different depths, touch different parts of her that fill her with delight at each thrust.

Each time I dive into her, I feel the tip of my cock, already beading up with precum, strike her g-spot and make her whole body twitch. I feel like I'm hammering away at the most sensitive buttons she has, and I have no intention of letting up. Being restrained makes it so much sweeter for her, so much more delicious to have my rock-hard, killer's body claiming her as mine.

We haven't used protection at any point. We don't want it.

Because Ana wants me to fill her with my thick, virile seed and put a child in her.

We've talked about it before, and while our first times together were just wild impulses, moments of carelessness, now we *want* it. And if my seed hasn't made her pregnant yet, we're going to keep trying until it happens. But I know, every time I fill her up, that she is as fertile and ready for more as the first night we spent together.

I feel her starting to tighten up again, and I start pounding harder. This is her favorite position--face in the sheets, hands bound behind her back, nothing to save her from my cock ravishing her g-spot deep inside her. It doesn't take her long to come, and she's already starting again.

"Oh god, Nikolai," she moans, and I feel her try to squirm, but I hold her tight. She can't escape me unless she says that magic safe word. "Oh god, I'm going to come!"

The next moment, I feel her going over the edge, and I let myself go.

My bucking gets wilder and more fierce, losing its machine-like precision and descending into unrestrained rutting. I get faster yet less precise, digging my fingers tighter into her, and suddenly, we reach our climax together.

Our groans fill the room together as shot after shot of my hot seed mixes with the honey that flows inside her as we convulse. She melts into the sheets, letting out a long, satisfied moan as my twitching cock empties itself inside her, filling her with those warm, familiar fluids that she loves so much.

I stay rock-hard, and she stays tight as ever, fitting my cock snugly and making sure to drain every last drop of my virile manhood from me.

Finally, it's over, and yet another page in the growing tome of our exploits comes to a close, leaving us in a room that has become heady with the scents of relentless lovemaking.

I pull out of her and gently remove her restraints before hugging her to me, spooning with her on the bed and peppering her neck with so many kisses that she laughs and squirms in my grasp. I massage her wrists where the bindings held her, and she gives me a satisfied murmur of delight as I press my still-hard cock against her ass.

"You know," I say, "I have a bottle of vodka imported from home with your name on it once we get this pregnancy in and over with."

She giggles and turns around to look into my eyes with her own shining gaze.

"I don't think we'll have to wait long for that," she says, rubbing her stomach. Even though we don't know for sure, I have a feeling she knows, and even that is enough to make me swell with pride. "But regardless," she adds with a mischievous smile, trailing off.

"Regardless...?" I ask.

"We'll have to make this official before I start showing," she finishes.

ANASTASIA

It has been a long few months. Trying to do anything good and pure in this world is difficult these days, and it's even harder when you're starting from a place of evil. The more I uncover about my father's legacy, the longer I stand in his position at the head of the Brighton Beach Bratva, the clearer it becomes to me just how neck-deep in crime and intrigue he really was. As it turns out, he didn't trust a single soul, not even Uncle Liev. They were friends of a shallow sort, more like enemies with a tenuous alliance between them. In addition to keeping me isolated and alone, I have figured out that another reason why he hired and fired so many staff members in quick succession was that he was incredibly paranoid. He never wanted to let any of them get too close. Once they began to worm their way in, most of them probably totally unaware that they were doing so, Daddy got nervous. He burned through them like matches. What a sad, empty life to lead: with nobody to confide in or care about. Not even me.

That has been one of the most difficult realizations to come to terms with: that my father, who I idolized for years, never truly loved me. Or if he did, it was in some sick, twisted, selfish way. Like he could see his own glory reflected in me because he helped create me. I was just another trophy for his cabinet, another jewel for his collection.

But it hardly matters now. Because I have love, real love, in my life now. Through all of the pain and the anxiety of taking up my father's filthy mantle, Nikolai has stood beside me, and when the situation calls for it, in front of me. He's not only my right hand man, but also my protector. My shield. I call the shots, but he advises me and does the legwork. He's not afraid of getting his hands dirty, especially now that it's always for a good cause. We have plans. Big, shiny, lofty plans to rebuild everything that my father broke. New York City is in turmoil. Everything is changing. But I think it's changing for the better.

The dirty money my father accrued through hurting people and destroying lives is now being funneled into programs to help bolster the community. We are rebuilding, not just metaphorically, but literally, as well. I am taking steps to legitimize all of our formerly criminal enterprises, turn them into above-board businesses with a conscience to guide them from here on out. Finally, I'm getting the opportunity to stretch my diplomatic muscles. I work alongside non-Bratva community leaders, including the mayor himself. Of course, there has been pushback from our associates. It's a monumental change between my father's rule and mine. But slowly I am proving to my people that we can do good *and* prosper. And those who refuse to walk into the light with me have no use to me whatsoever. I have already had to prune our hedges, so to speak, of parasites and pests. Nikolai handles that himself pretty damn well. Having a hitman on my side is just about the best backup a girl could ask for.

He will always protect me, and right now, I need protecting more than ever. Because I'm pregnant, and just barely starting to show. Right now, the two- - or three-- of us are holed up in my father's old mansion at Sands Point, lying low and relaxing in between two big publicity stunts to raise money for the struggling infrastructure out here on the island. We're doing good work, and I'm grateful, but right now I need a rest. I'm lying on my childhood bed, my head resting in Nikolai's lap, while he softly strokes my hair. There's an old classic rock record playing downstairs, and the summer breeze rolls in through the partially-opened window, carrying faint scents of rose and jasmine from the garden. It's late afternoon, and Nikolai is nursing a vodka tonic. As much as I wish I could join him, I've got a precious little soul growing inside me, so I'm sipping herbal tea instead.

"Things are going to get harder before they get easier, aren't they?" I ask suddenly.

Nikolai looks down at me and smiles, nodding. "*Da*, my love. That's the way it goes."

"I hope we can handle it. It's a lot of work, trying to save the city. Especially with a baby on the way," I add, gently rubbing my belly.

"You're right. It won't ever be simple, but it will smooth out over time. Together, we have already made good things happen. We're a good team, Ana," he tells me honestly. He leans down to kiss me, and I smile.

"Despite everything, I'm happy," I admit. "It's a fucked-up world, but this part-- this little corner of it-- is perfect. You and me, together. I love you, Nikolai, and I can't wait to see what the future holds for the three of us."

"I love you, too," he says, making my heart skip a beat. No matter how many times he tells me, it never stops giving me a little thrill of delight. "You and I are going to make the world a better place. A safer place. And not just for everyone else, but for us. For our baby."

"It'll be hard work, but we can do it," I agree.

"And we've got the rest of our lives to work on it,

because I'm not going anywhere, Anastasia. From the moment I laid eyes on you at that airport, from the moment you fell into my arms at the Ovechkin mansion, I knew I would never leave you. You're stuck with me, *lyubov moya*, now and forever."

"Good," I answer, grinning. "Because I don't ever want to imagine my life without you."

Nikolai bends down to kiss me, more sensually this time, whispering, "And you will never have to, my love. Not as long as my heart is still beating. I'm yours, and you are mine."

THANK you so much for reading! I hope you enjoyed <3 If you have a moment, please leave a review. Other readers are dying to know what you thought.

I have plenty more bad boy romance for you, so make sure you check out my other books on the next couple of pages, and sign up for my newsletter to be notified when I have a new release on the way!

~Alexis Abbott

Killing For Her

Abducted

STEPBROTHERS:

Ruthless

Criminal

STANDALONES:

Betting on Love

Hunter's Baby

I Hired A Hitman

Vegas Boss

Rock Hard Bodyguard

Innocence For Sale: Jane

Redeeming Viktor

Romance:

Falling for her Boss (Novella)

Most Wanted: Lilly (Novella)

Bound as the World Burns (SFF)

Erotic Thriller:

THE DANGEROUS MEN SERIES:

The Narrow Path

Strayed from the Path

Path to Ruin

ABOUT THE AUTHOR

Alexis Abbott is a Wall Street Journal & USA Today bestselling author who writes about bad boys protecting their girls! Pick up her books today if you can't resist a bad boy who is a good man, and find yourself transported with super steamy sex, gritty suspense, and lots of romance.

She lives in beautiful St. John's, NL, Canada with her amazing husband.

facebook.com/abbottauthor

twitter.com/abbottauthor

instagram.com/alexisabbottauthor

bookbub.com/authors/alexis-abbott

pinterest.com/badboyromance

youtube.com/AlexisAbbott

ACKNOWLEDGMENTS

Thank you to my amazing Patrons. I'm constantly humbled and grateful for your support.

Ramona Cabrera
Melissa Hedrick
Virginia Swanson
Dawn Daughenbaugh
Don Doss
Stacie Currie

If you'd like to join them — and get my ebooks or paperbacks — you can find me here on Patreon.
https://www.patreon.com/alexisabbott